THE SCENT OF ALMONDS
& OTHER STORIES

Camilla Lackberg is a worldwide bestseller renowned for her brilliant contemporary psychological thrillers. Her novels have sold over 12 million copies in 55 countries with translations into 37 languages.

www.CamillaLackberg.com

Also by Camilla Lackberg

CAMILLA LACKBERG

THE SCENT OF ALMONDS & OTHER STORIES

Translated from the Swedish by
Tiina Nunnally

HARPER

Harper
An imprint of HarperCollins*Publishers*
1 London Bridge Street,
London SE1 9GF

www.harpercollins.co.uk

Published by HarperCollins*Publishers* 2015
1

A catalogue record for this book
is available from the British Library

ISBN: 978-0-00-747907-8

This novel is entirely a work of fiction.
The names, characters and incidents portrayed in it are
the work of the author's imagination. Any resemblance to
actual persons, living or dead, events or localities is
entirely coincidental.

Set in Meridien by Palimpsest Book Production Ltd, Falkirk, Stirlingshire

Printed and bound in Great Britain by
Clays Ltd, St Ives plc

MIX
Paper from
responsible sources
FSC C007454

FSC™ is a non-profit international organisation established to promote
the responsible management of the world's forests. Products carrying the
FSC label are independently certified to assure consumers that they come
from forests that are managed to meet the social, economic and
ecological needs of present and future generations,
and other controlled sources.

Find out more about HarperCollins and the environment at
www.harpercollins.co.uk/green

CONTENTS

THE SCENT OF ALMONDS

Snow drifted through the air. Christmas was only a week away, and December had already racked up a record amount of snow and freezing cold temperatures. The ice had set in several weeks ago, but over the past few days a thaw had turned it brittle and unreliable.

Martin Molin was standing in the bow of the boat as it ploughed its way forward, following in the path forged by the coastguard cutter out to Valö. He wondered what he was doing here, and whether he'd made the right decision. But Lisette had been so insistent. To be honest, she had begged him to come. Family gatherings were not her strong suit, she'd said, and it would be much easier to bear if he were there to keep her company. The problem was that meeting her relatives implied a certain seriousness about their relationship that he, at least, didn't feel.

But what was done was done. And what was

1

said was said. Now here he was, on his way out to the old summer camp on Valö to spend two days with her family.

He looked back over his shoulder. Fjällbacka was undeniably beautiful, especially in the winter with the small wooden buildings nestled amid all that whiteness. And the way in which the little community was embraced by the grey mountain gave it a unique and aesthetically appealing air of drama. Maybe I should move here from Tanumshede, Martin thought briefly, but then laughed at himself. That would only happen if he won the lottery.

'Toss me the painter, would you?' shouted the man on the dock, startling Martin out of his reveries. He leaned down to pick up the line lying at his feet. When the boat got close enough, he threw it over the rail. The man easily caught the line and tied it to the bollard.

'You're the last one to arrive. The other guests are already here.'

Martin cautiously stepped down onto the slippery dock to shake hands with the man.

'There were a few things I had to finish at the station before I could leave.'

'Right. I heard that we were going to have a police presence out here this weekend. Makes me feel very safe.'

The man laughed and then introduced himself as Börje, the owner of the hotel.

'My wife and I run the place. So I'm the

2

carpenter, cook, butler and general handyman. All in one.' Another loud, resounding laugh.

Martin picked up his bag and followed Börje towards the lights that could be glimpsed through the trees. 'From what I've heard, you've done wonders with the old camp,' he said.

'We've put in a lot of work,' said Börje proudly. 'And money – I have to admit that. But now it's doing well. The wife and I have been very pleased. We were actually fully booked all summer and well into the autumn. And we've been surprised to see that the Christmas special we're offering has proved to be so popular.'

'People like to get away from all the Christmas hubbub,' said Martin, trying not to pant too much as they trudged up the hill towards the hotel. It was embarrassing; he ought to be in better shape, considering his age and his profession.

He took his eyes off the path and looked up, momentarily stunned. They really had done wonders with the old building. Like most people who had grown up in the area, Martin had come out to Valö on school field trips or to attend summer camp. He remembered a beautiful but somewhat run-down green building situated in the middle of an expansive lawn. Now the green paint had been replaced with white, and the structure gleamed like a jewel. From the windows streamed a warm light that made the white facade glow. Torches burned in front of the entrance, and through the windows on the ground floor he could see a huge Christmas tree. The whole place was incredibly beautiful, and he paused for a moment to take it all in.

'Quite spectacular, don't you think?' Börje had also stopped.

'Incredible,' said Martin, and he meant it.

They went in through the main entrance and stomped their feet to shake off the snow.

'The last guest has arrived!' called Börje, his voice echoing down the hall. Martin heard quick footsteps as someone approached.

'Martin! You're here! It's so good to see you!' Lisette threw her arms around his neck, and again he had the feeling that he really shouldn't have come. She was nice, and he found her attractive. Yet he was starting to think that she viewed their relationship as a bigger deal than he did. But it was too late for regrets. What mattered now was making it through the weekend.

'Come with me!' Lisette took his hand and more or less dragged him into the big room on the left. In Martin's memories from his childhood, this had once been a dorm room crowded with bunk beds. Now it had been meticulously transformed into a living-room-cum-library. In the middle towered the giant Christmas tree, decorated according to the latest artistic trends.

'Here he is!' exclaimed Lisette triumphantly. Her relatives all turned to stare at Martin. He resisted an urge to tug at his shirt collar and instead gave a rather comical wave. When Lisette poked him in the side, he realized that something more was apparently expected of him, so he began methodically making his way around the room, moving from left to right. Lisette accompanied him so that she could introduce each person as they shook hands.

'This is my father, Harald.' A large man with bushy hair and an equally bushy moustache stood up to shake Martin's hand with great energy.

'And this is my mother, Britten.'

'My name is actually Britt-Marie, but nobody has called me anything but Britten ever since I was five years old.' Lisette's mother also stood up to greet him, and Martin was struck by how alike the mother and daughter were. The same trim figure, the same nut-brown eyes and dark hair, even though Britten's had quite a few streaks of grey.

'How wonderful to meet you at last,' said Lisette's mother as she sat down.

Martin murmured something similar in reply, hoping the white lie wasn't too obvious.

'And here is Uncle Gustav,' said Lisette. It was clear from her expression that this shorter and skinnier version of her father was not among her favourite relatives.

'My pleasure, my pleasure,' said Gustav Liljecrona politely, even offering a slight bow. Martin wondered if he was expected to bow in return, but decided that a brief nod would suffice. Gustav's wife, who was the next person in line, also failed to evoke any genuine regard from Lisette, judging by her tone of voice.

'My aunt, Vivi.'

Martin grasped a dry, shrivelled hand. A hand that was in sharp contrast to the woman's face, which was so devoid of wrinkles that her skin seemed to be stretched as taut as the head of a drum. He was convinced that he'd see the traces of multiple surgical procedures if he tried to look behind her ears, but he managed to resist the impulse.

Clearly there was more familial affection between Lisette and the man sitting next to Aunt Vivi, since she announced 'my cousin, Bernard' with both warmth and joy. Yet Martin felt an instinctive dislike for the elegantly dressed man in his thirties. His hair was slicked back in the style that for some inexplicable reason was so popular among members of the financial sector.

'So, this is Lisette's policeman,' he smirked, sounding like a real Stockholmer. Even though the statement was both correct and highly innocuous, Martin sensed that something else was lurking under the man's nonchalant tone. Something derogatory, though he couldn't quite put his finger on it.

'That's right,' he replied, shifting his gaze to the young woman next to Cousin Bernard.

'Bernard's sister, Miranda,' Lisette told Martin, who couldn't help feeling startled as he took her outstretched hand. Cousin Miranda was breath-takingly beautiful. About twenty-five or so, with the same pitch-black hair as her brother, although her tresses were longer, and with dazzling blue eyes that she now fixed on Martin. For a moment he lost all focus. A slight cough from Lisette made him realize that he may have held on to her cousin's hand too long, and he let go as if he'd burned himself.

'My brother, Mattias. Although everyone calls him Matte,' said Lisette with ice in her voice. Martin hurried to shift his attention to Lisette's older brother. He had an open and pleasant face, and he shook Martin's hand with enthusiasm.

'I've heard so much about you. Lisette has hardly talked about anybody else since summer. It's very, very nice to meet you finally.'

A dramatic pause followed, and then Lisette said:

'Last but not least – Grandpa Ruben.'

Martin found himself standing in front of an elderly man seated in a wheelchair. Ruben passed on his facial features to both sons, but over time he had shrunk to the size of a child. A checked blanket covered his lap and legs as he sat in his wheelchair. Yet his handshake was surprisingly strong, his eyes alert.

'So . . . this is your young man,' he said with an amused expression. Martin felt like a schoolboy standing before the headmaster. There was something extremely impressive about the old man, and Martin was familiar with his story. Ruben had been born as poor as a church mouse. From nothing he'd built an empire that today earned billions all around the world. It was a story that most Swedes knew.

'Time for dinner!' said a woman's voice from the doorway, and everyone turned in that direction. A woman wearing an old-fashioned white apron stood there, motioning towards the dining room. Martin assumed she was Börje's wife.

'Good. I could use some food about now,' said Harald, immediately heading for the table. The others followed close behind, and Martin watched with amusement as several family members rushed for Ruben's wheelchair, battling to get there first. Lisette, who was the closest, emerged victorious, casting a triumphant glance at Aunt Vivi. Obviously there were some underlying family conflicts that he, the outsider, knew nothing about. Again he sighed. It was going to be a very long weekend.

Lisette felt the others staring at her as she pushed Grandpa Ruben's wheelchair towards the dining room. Her successful effort made her cheeks flush, and she hoped that this minor victory was an indication of who would emerge the winner from the bigger battle: the one being fought over her grandfather's money. Sometimes she felt almost dizzy at the thought of how much money would one day be hers. It wasn't a question of millions, but rather billions of Swedish kronor. What mattered now was staying close to the old man and hoping that the others would make fools of themselves, one after the other – which wasn't all that unlikely.

She knew for a fact that her father and uncle were on the verge of burning their bridges; neither would prove much of an obstacle. Nor would Bernard and Miranda, for that matter. No, her strongest competitor for the inheritance was Matte. As things stood, she had to admit that he was her grandfather's favourite. Even more than she was. But she was convinced that was only temporary. All she had to do was bide her time, and Matte would no doubt reveal some weakness that she'd be able to exploit.

'Oh, I'm so sorry!' She had just pushed the wheelchair into Martin's shin, and she stopped to let him pass. For a moment she wondered whether it had been a good idea to invite him. But she'd been so determined to show her grandfather that she was now a mature adult, and having a steady boyfriend who also happened to be a police officer suited the image perfectly. Yet she wished Martin hadn't behaved in such a clumsy manner when she introduced him to everyone. It took only one glance at Bernard to see what he thought of her boyfriend, and she suspected the others shared his opinion. Martin was a nice person, and very sweet, but it was obvious that he wasn't exactly a man of the world. Well, she'd simply have to make the best of the situation in order to survive the weekend. She pushed her grandfather's wheelchair into the dining room.

The sight of all the food piled up on platters on the sideboard was overwhelming. A vast array of mouth-watering offerings: ham, spiced pork roll, herring salad, pickled herring, meatballs, small sausages, and so on. Everything that anyone could want from a Christmas buffet, and Martin was embarrassed to hear his stomach growling loudly.

'Sounds like the boy is hungry,' laughed Harald, slapping Martin on the back.

'You're right. I suppose I am,' he replied with a strained smile. He hoped to God that Lisette's father wouldn't make a habit of calling him 'the boy' and slapping him on the back.

A short time later everyone had filled their plates and then taken seats at the beautifully set dining-room table. Outside the window the snowfall had increased, turning into almost blizzard-like condi-tions. As Börje moved around the table pouring cold schnapps into everyone's glass, he seemed worried.

'It's not looking good. According to the weather forecast, we're in for a real storm. It may be difficult for anyone to reach the mainland if they have to,' he said, nodding at the snow outside.

'That won't be necessary,' said Ruben in his dry, old-man's voice. 'We're not planning to go anywhere until Sunday, and we're certainly not going to starve.'

Everyone laughed at his remark. A bit too loudly, a bit too heartily. A disapproving furrow appeared between Ruben's bushy eyebrows. He's probably sick and tired of everyone fawning over him, thought Martin. For a second they exchanged glances, and Martin realized that the old man was aware of what he was thinking. He lowered his eyes and focused on spreading a dab of mustard on one of the little sausages that curled up at either end. When he was a kid, Martin had called them 'permed' sausages, which was something his parents still reminded him of every Christmas when he visited them.

'So, Bernard,' said Ruben, shifting his attention to his grandson. 'How's the firm doing these days? I've heard a number of rumours lately.'

A few seconds of oppressive silence ensued before Bernard replied.

'Nothing but spiteful gossip. Business is better than ever.'

'Is that so? That's not what I've been hearing,' said Ruben. 'And my sources – as you well know – are considered highly reliable.'

'No offence to your sources, Grandpa Ruben, but I can imagine that they may not be in the thick of things any longer. So what would they know about . . .'

A sharp look from Vivi made Bernard fall silent. Speaking in a somewhat less aggressive tone, he said: 'All I can say is that your sources are wrong. We're going to show excellent results in the next quarter.'

'And what about you, Miranda? How's it going with your design company?' Ruben's eyes were as piercing as X-rays, and Miranda squirmed as she answered the question.

'Er, well, we've had a bit of bad luck. A number of orders have been cancelled of late, and we've had to do a few jobs pro bono in order to establish customer references, and—'

Ruben held up his bony hand. 'Okay, thanks, that's enough. I get the picture. In other words, there's not much left of the capital that I invested. Am I right?'

'Um . . . well, you see, Grandpa, I was planning to talk to you about that . . .' She twirled a strand of her lovely dark hair around her finger as she gave the old man an ingratiating smile.

'The children are so clever and they work so hard,' said Vivi, trying to rescue the situation. Tugging nervously at her pearl necklace, she babbled on: 'Lately, Gustav and I hardly ever see them at home. They're always working, working, working . . .'

The bits of sausage started to swell inside Martin's mouth. The conversation had taken an unpleasant turn, and he tried to catch Lisette's eye. Like the other family members, she was sitting at the table in tense anticipation, greedily following the exchange of words.

'Any plans to start working sometime soon, Lisette?'

Lisette found herself stumbling for something to say as her grandfather suddenly focused his attention on her.

'I'm . . . I'm . . . well, you know, I'm studying,' she stammered nervously as she seemed to shrink in her chair.

'Yes, I do know that,' replied Ruben drily. 'I'm

the one financing your studies. And have been for eight years now. I wonder whether it isn't time for you to put some of that knowledge into practice.' His tone was deceptively gentle, but Lisette kept her frightened gaze on her lap as she murmured, 'Yes, Grandpa.' He snorted and then turned to his sons.

'Having some problems at work, I hear.'

Martin saw Harald and Gustav quickly exchange glances. A wordless communication that lasted all of a second, but in that moment Martin was able to read both hatred and alarm.

'What have you heard, Father?' Harald said at last, accompanying the question with a big but superficial smile. It was his hands that betrayed his true feelings, manically tearing the napkin to shreds as he talked.

'Everything's going smoothly, as always. Business as usual, you know. Just like in your day.'

'My day,' grunted Ruben. 'You know quite well that "my day" was no more than two years ago. You make it sound as if a hundred years has passed since I stood at the helm. And if I hadn't developed these . . .' he searched for the right words '. . . health problems, I'd still be standing there. But I have my sources within the company. And I've heard some things that are very disturbing.' He shook his finger as he looked from Harald to Gustav.

Prompted by an urgent glance from Harald, Gustav cleared his throat and spoke. 'As Harald said, everything is fine. I don't know what you may have heard—'

Again Ruben grunted and saliva spewed from his mouth as he exclaimed: 'What a sorry lot you are! All your lives you've been holding on to my coat-tails, spending my money, expecting to receive a silver spoon the minute you open your mouths! And against my better judgement I've given you countless opportunities. I've handed out more and more money for your enterprises, and I've allowed you' – he indicated his two sons – 'to take charge of my company, because I wanted so dearly to have the firm stay in the family. But you've all betrayed me! You've misappropriated and squandered and diminished everything I've ever given to you. And now I've had enough!'

Ruben slammed his fist on the table, making everyone jump. Martin knew that he should flee from this unpleasant situation he'd found himself in, yet he had the same feeling as if he'd happened upon a traffic accident. He just couldn't tear his eyes away.

'It's my intention to disinherit every single one of you! I've rewritten my will, and it's ready to be signed and witnessed. You'll get no more than I am legally obliged to give you. A number of carefully chosen charities will thank their lucky stars, come the day I kick the bucket – because they'll be getting the bulk of my fortune!'

The whole family stared at the man in the wheelchair. It looked as if someone had hit pause and frozen the tableau, because not one person moved. There wasn't a sound in the room except for Ruben's laboured breathing and the storm outside that now pounded like a wild animal on the windowpanes.

His outburst must have made Ruben thirsty, because he raised his water glass with a trembling hand and greedily drank every drop. Still no one spoke, no one moved. Ruben set down his glass, looking as if the air were slowly seeping out of him, like a punctured balloon.

A slight tremor in his face was the first warning that something was wrong, followed by a faint twitching on the right side, which rapidly moved to the left. Spasms began rippling through his body. To begin with they were barely noticeable, but they quickly intensified. A guttural sound issued from his throat, and then his whole, wizened frame started shaking as he sat in his chair. At that point the others reacted.

'Grandpa!' shrieked Lisette, throwing herself towards him.

Bernard also leapt to his feet, but both of them hesitated, unsure what to do. Bernard gripped Ruben's scrawny shoulders, but the spasms were so strong that he couldn't hold the old man still.

'He's dying, he's dying!' screamed Vivi, yanking so hard on her pearl necklace that the string broke and pearls cascaded all over the floor.

'Do something!' shouted Britten, looking around helplessly.

Martin rushed towards Ruben, but no sooner

did he reach the old man's side than the spasms abruptly stopped. Ruben's body fell forward until his face landed in his plate with a nasty thud. Placing his thumb and index finger on the man's wrist, Martin felt for a pulse, but after a moment he was forced to say:

'He's dead. I'm sorry.'

Vivi screamed again as she fumbled for the necklace, which was no longer in place.

Börje and his wife came running from the kitchen, and Harald shouted to them:

'Ring the coastguard – we need an ambulance! My father has had some sort of seizure. We need to get help!'

Börje shook his head gloomily. 'I'm afraid the storm has brought down the phone lines. I tried to make a call a little while ago, but the phone wasn't working.'

'Unfortunately, it wouldn't make any difference,' said Martin, getting to his feet. 'As I said, he's already dead.'

'But what happened?' sobbed Britten. 'Did he have a heart attack? A stroke? What happened?'

Martin was about to shrug, to indicate that he had no idea. But then he caught a whiff of something in the air. A smell that seemed to hover around the old man's place at the table. A smell that Martin thought he recognized. He leaned over Ruben, whose face was still resting among the herring and meatballs, and sniffed harder. Yes, there it was. Faint, but distinct. The scent of almonds. A smell that should not have been there. Martin reached for Ruben's glass and held it up to his nose. The clear scent of bitter almonds rose to his nostrils and confirmed his suspicions.

'He was murdered.'

Her heart was pounding as she stared at the top of Grandpa Ruben's head. He was so still.

Miranda clutched the edge of the table, unable to take her eyes off the dead man. But the anger she'd felt at his outburst hadn't yet faded, and she had to fight off an urge to kick him in the shins. How dare he attack her like that! And in front of everyone. Not just her immediate family but also the cousins and her aunt and uncle, who had stared at her like hungry wolves, ready to grab what was left after the alpha-male had eaten his fill.

Why couldn't Ruben have given her more time? Of all people, he ought to know how long it took to build a company from the ground up. They should have been able to resolve this matter. After all, he still had plenty of money. He wouldn't have even missed another couple of million kronor – that was pocket change to him. And poor Bernard. He didn't deserve to be flayed like that either. He worked so hard, and he really had every chance of making a go of things. All he needed was a little more time . . . And money.

Good Lord! What if the old man had already changed his will? The thought struck Miranda with such force that she had to gasp for breath. Her fingernails dug even harder into the wood of the table, and she felt tears spring to her eyes. He might have contacted his lawyer and made all the changes before the weekend. In fact, that was probably what he'd done. She was convinced that Ruben was sly and malicious enough to have done exactly that. He'd have enjoyed nothing better than watching them fuss over him before delivering the coup de grâce.

He was legally obligated to leave to them a certain amount from his estate, but once the sums that he'd already given them were subtracted, there would be very little left for each family member. Was it possible that they might even end up owing money? And she was up to her ears in debt as things stood! Miranda could feel the air getting harder to breathe. Angrily she glared at the murdered man in the wheelchair.

The rest of the evening proceeded as if in a fog. Initially Martin's pronouncement caused a deafening silence to descend upon the room. A moment later it unleashed a cacophony of objections. No one wanted to believe him, so Martin had calmly explained that the scent of bitter almonds was a strong indication that cyanide had been present. Moreover Ruben's seizure matched the effects of that extremely potent poison.

He asked Börje for a paper sack in which he carefully placed Ruben's water glass so that it could be sent to the lab for analysis. Martin was mortified that he'd handled the glass without a second thought, possibly destroying fingerprints that could be valuable to the investigation.

'We need to get this over to the mainland,' Martin told Börje in an authoritative voice. In his mind he'd already started making a list of what measures needed to be taken. Notify his colleagues at the police station. Gather evidence. Ensure that the victim's body was sent to the pathology lab. And, most importantly, begin interviewing the witnesses. If only they could return to the mainland quickly, the whole process of finding the killer could get underway.

'That won't be possible,' said Börje quietly, indicating the storm raging outside the windows. The snow was now coming down so hard that they seemed to be looking at a wall of white.

'What do you mean it "won't be possible"?' asked Martin, frustrated. 'We need to get back to the mainland.'

'Not in this weather. That's not going to happen.' Börje threw out his hands helplessly.

'But it's not that far.' Martin could hear how annoyed he sounded, so he told himself to calm down. He, more than anyone else, needed to keep his composure.

'Börje's right,' said his wife. 'A boat would never make it across. The wind is blowing towards the dock, and in a gale of this force, we wouldn't stand a chance. No, we're just going to have to wait for the storm to subside.'

'Then we must ring the coastguard,' said Martin resolutely.

'The phone's not working.' replied Bernard. His tone of voice clearly signalled that he considered Martin to be an idiot.

'But we've got mobile phones.' Martin pulled his mobile out of his pocket, but his heart sank when he saw there wasn't even one bar on the display. No reception.

'Bloody hell!' he shouted. It took all the self-control he could muster to keep from hurling his phone against the wall.

'I told you so,' remarked Bernard with a barely concealed grin that made Martin want to punch him.

'Do you mean we're all stuck here?' Miranda whined as she clung to Matte's arm. He didn't seem to notice her. His eyes were filled with tears as he stared at the dead man slumped over the table.

For the first time it struck Martin that Matte was the only person seated at the table who had not been subjected to the old man's demeaning questions. He was also the only one who now showed any sign of grief. As if to confirm what Martin was thinking, Matte got up and went over to the old man. He lifted Ruben's face from the plate and began wiping it with a cloth napkin. Everyone stared at Matte as if hypnotized, but nobody made any attempt to help. When Ruben's face was clean, Matte gently leaned his body back in the wheelchair and straightened the blanket that covered his lap.

'Thank you, Matte,' said Britten, giving her son a warm glance.

'We need to put him somewhere cold,' said Martin, trying to avoid looking at Matte. 'If we're not going to be able to leave, then we have to preserve . . . the evidence.' He was expressing himself clumsily, but for the time being he was the only one who could safeguard the investigation and minimize the damage as much as possible. Someone in this house was a killer, and he had no intention of letting that person get away.

'We can put him in the cold-storage room,' said Börje, stepping forward to help.

'Good,' replied Martin curtly.

Transporting the victim was made easier thanks to the wheelchair, and Martin was able to push it all the way inside the cold store.

'Is it possible to lock the door?' he asked Börje, who nodded and pointed to a padlock hanging on the wall.

'We don't want to catch our guests swiping any steaks,' he explained with a wry smile, which quickly faded when Martin did not respond.

After locking Ruben's body inside, Martin and Börje returned to the dining room. Everyone was still seated exactly where they had been when Martin left them a few minutes earlier. No one seemed capable of moving.

'Let's go into the library,' said Martin, gesturing towards the room at the other end of the hall. 'Börje, is there any cognac?' The hotel owner nodded and went to fetch a bottle. 'Could you please make a fire in the fireplace . . .' He searched his memory for the name of Börje's wife but realized he'd only heard her referred to as 'the wife'.

'Kerstin. My name is Kerstin,' she told him. 'And yes, of course. I'd be happy to do that.'

She too disappeared, and Martin turned his gaze to the members of the Liljecrona family. Not one person had so much as moved a muscle.

'All right. Let's go. Come with me.' He led the way, expecting them to follow.

One by one they entered the library and sat down. Kerstin was busy lighting the fire, and by the time everyone had taken a seat Börje came running in with a bottle of cognac. He took cognac glasses from a cabinet and poured a generous amount of the liquor in each one.

'Is this standard practice for police in the area? Plying the witnesses with drink?' asked Gustav in a low voice. But he gratefully accepted the glass that Börje offered him, and a moment later he held it out for a refill.

'I wouldn't exactly say that,' replied Martin with a wan smile. 'But nothing about this situation is standard. We'll just have to proceed as best we can.' He wished that Patrik Hedström, his closest colleague at the Tanumshede police station, were present. Martin hadn't worked with Patrik for very long, but he admired him tremendously. He would have felt more confident if Patrik were here. His colleague would have undoubtedly known what to do. But as things stood, Martin would have to handle the situation on his own. And he had no intention of disappointing Patrik. He told himself it was simply a matter of relying on common sense and taking one thing at a time.

'Since we can't get to the police station, I'll have to take your statements here. I want to speak to each of you individually, and I assume that you're all willing to cooperate so that we can get to the bottom of what just happened.' He looked at each family member in turn; no one seemed inclined to offer any objections.

'Then I suggest you and I begin.' Martin nodded at Harald.

Her hand shook as she held the glass of cognac. With a worried expression she fixed her eyes on her husband's broad back as he left the library. She was nervous about his health. Nervous about how he'd handle the pressure. Harald looked so strong, so solid, but Britten knew that it was all a facade. Long years of marriage had taught her that her big, boisterous husband was still just a frightened little boy. And she blamed Ruben for that. He'd been too harsh, demanded too much, expected his sons to be made of the same stuff as he was. Neither of them was. Gustav at least looked weak, and so he tended to get off comparatively lightly. Harald, on the other hand, had always given the impression of strength and power by virtue of his size, and no one had ever realized how weak he was inside. Well, maybe Ruben had done, deep in his heart. But he had chosen to close his eyes to the truth, and for that Britten had hated him.

The job he'd given to Harald was doomed to failure from the very start. And the thought of allowing Gustav and Harald to work together . . . It was such an absurd idea that she wondered whether Ruben was in his right mind when he proposed the plan. Naturally his sons had taken the bait. They were so eager for approval that their tongues were practically hanging out of their mouths, drooling with the desire to show their father that they were worthy of his trust. All past failures would be wiped away in one fell swoop. This was their chance; finally, after all these years, they would win their father's respect. Maybe even his love. That was what the two brothers had dared to hope for. Instead, the arrangement had turned out to be a complete disaster. Britten had watched Harald come home from the office, his face turning greyer and greyer each day. Looking more and more defeated. The heart attack he'd suffered a year ago had come as no surprise. Thankfully, Harald had survived. At that point his father should have realized that the job was too much for his son. But he hadn't. Ruben had sent a bouquet of flowers to Harald's sickbed and the very next day asked him when he'd be ready to return to work.

'What do you think he's going to say?' Gustav whispered to Britten. 'Do you think he'll—'

'I don't know, Gustav,' she replied tersely. There

was something about her brother-in-law's constant whining and timid manner that made her tense up in irritation.

'I really hope that he doesn't . . .' That plaintive voice again, this time a bit shriller. 'I really hope that he—'

'Stop it!' Britten's tone, more than her words, made him halt mid-sentence. 'It doesn't matter what Harald says or doesn't say. A line has been crossed, and now it's as well that everything come out.'

'But . . .' Gustav ventured, his eyes flitting about nervously.

Britten, however, had had enough. She turned her back on him and gazed out of the window at the snowstorm. There was nothing more to discuss.

'I understand that you're the older son.'

'Yes.' Harald Liljecrona stared straight ahead, his face expressionless. They'd been given permission to borrow the office belonging to Börje and Kerstin, and the two men were now seated on either side of the cluttered desk. Kerstin had helped Martin find an unused notepad and a pen, so he was ready to jot down whatever information he was able to obtain. He would have preferred to use a tape recorder, as they did at the police station, but he would just have to make do with what was available.

'Yes, I'm the older son,' Harald repeated, turning to look at Martin.

'And you are employed by the family business, is that correct?'

Harald laughed. His laugh sounded a bit comical and much too high-pitched for a man of such impressive girth. 'Right. If you can call a world-wide enterprise dealing in billions of kronor a "family business".'

'And what exactly is your role?' Martin was looking at him intently.

'I'm the CEO. Gustav is the financial director.'

'Do the two of you work well together?'

Again that peculiar laugh. 'It may not have been one of Father's best ideas to give us overlapping areas of responsibility. My brother and I have never got on well and there's no use pretending otherwise. I dare say you'll hear about it from the rest of the family, especially Vivi. Her tongue was made for spreading gossip . . .' He paused for a moment and then continued. 'Maybe Father was hoping that Gustav and I would grow closer if we were forced to work together on a daily basis. Instead, it made the situation worse.'

'Was there something in particular Ruben was referring to at dinner when he asked you how the company was going?'

This time Harald didn't laugh.

'I have no idea what he was talking about. It's true that Gustav and I seldom agree about anything, and at the office we occasionally throw a few plates at one another – metaphorically speaking, of course. But I don't understand what Father could have heard that would prompt him to make such a comment.'

'You have no idea?'

'No,' said Harald in a low voice, clearly indicating that he had no intention of supplying any more information pertaining to that line of enquiry. Not even if there were other things he could have mentioned.

'Do you have any theories as to who might have wanted to kill your father?' asked Martin, waiting tensely for the answer as his pen hovered over the notepad.

'Well, you heard for yourself what went on at the dinner table. Which one of those vultures wouldn't want to kill him?' The words spilled out spontaneously, but then Harald seemed to regret what he'd said.

'It's not really that bad. I mean, we've had our family quarrels and arguments – I won't deny that. But for someone to make the leap to actually murder him? No, I have no idea.'

Martin asked a few more questions before ending the interview when he realized that he wasn't going to get any further.

Miranda was the next person to take a seat opposite Martin. He had no particular system regarding the order in which he talked to the family members, his primary concern was simply to interview all of them.

She looked small and fragile as she sat across

from him. She had pulled her dark hair back into a tight ponytail, which further enhanced her beautiful face.

'It's so awful,' she said, her lower lip quivering. Martin had to restrain an urge to put his arms around her and tell her that everything was going to be all right. He was annoyed with himself. That sort of reaction was totally unprofessional.

'Yes, it certainly is,' he said instead as he lightly tapped his pen on the notepad. 'What can you tell me about who might be a suspect in your grandfather's death?'

'Nothing. Absolutely nothing,' sobbed Miranda. 'I don't understand how this could have happened! How could anyone do something so horrible?'

With some embarrassment Martin handed her a tissue from the box on top of the desk. Weeping women always made him uncomfortable. He cleared his throat.

'From what I gathered at dinner, your grandfather was not especially pleased with the way all of you have handled your finances.' He could hear how stilted his words sounded.

'Grandpa has always been so generous towards his children and grandchildren,' she said, still crying. 'He loaned me the funds I needed to start my design company, and if only I'd had a little more time . . . and maybe a little more money, I know I could have made it a success. But I've had such terrible bad luck along the way, and the customers have never really discovered my work, and . . .' Her words gave way to sobbing.

'So your grandfather loaned you some money. And now it's all gone, and you were thinking of asking him for more? Is that correct?'

Miranda nodded. 'Yes. I only needed a million. That would have given me the necessary time to make a go of things. The fashion industry is tough, and you have to take big risks if you want to succeed.' She tossed her head, and her lip stopped quivering.

'So you were planning to ask your grandfather for a million kronor?'

'Yes.' Again that stubborn toss of the head. 'That's pocket change for him. Do you have any idea how much the old man had in the bank?' She rolled her eyes but then realized what she'd just said. Again her lip started quivering.

'But you hadn't yet asked him for the loan?' Martin now felt considerably less sympathy for the woman as he watched the crocodile tears rolling down her cheeks.

'No, no,' she assured him, leaning forward. 'I was planning to ask him during the weekend.'

'What about the other family members?'

'What do you mean? What about them?'

'Ruben seemed to have strong opinions about them as well. Do you think any of them might have had a more violent response than—'

Miranda cut him off. Her eyes were flashing with anger.

'Do you seriously imagine I would sit here and

accuse a member of my own family of murder? Is that what you think? Is it?'

'I merely asked whether anyone might have had a more violent response than the rest of the family.'

'But isn't that the same thing as asking me who I think killed Grandpa?' replied Miranda coldly.

Martin had to admit to himself that she was right. He suddenly felt extremely tired. For weeks he'd been dreading coming out here with Lisette, and he could now say that everything had turned out a hundred times worse than he could possibly have imagined. He glanced at his watch. It was gone eleven p.m.

'I think we'll stop here,' he said. 'It's getting late. We'll continue tomorrow.'

A relieved expression appeared on Miranda's face. But she merely nodded as she got to her feet. Martin followed her into the library to speak to the others. The mood was so oppressive that he almost felt as if he'd walked into a wall.

'I'm going to stop the interviews for tonight. I know everyone is tired, and I think it would be more productive to continue in the morning, after we've all had some rest.'

No one replied, but everyone looked relieved.

'Would you like a cognac?' asked Lisette as she came over to Martin and put her hand on his arm. His first instinct was to decline. In a practical sense, he was officially on duty. But exhaustion and the weight of responsibility had taken their toll, and he found himself nodding as he sank into the nearest armchair. Outside, the snow was still coming down hard. A branch could be heard banging against a windowpane at the other end of the building.

'Is it true that we can't get over to the mainland?' Vivi's voice broke, and her hand shook as she again raised it to her neck where her pearls had been.

'Didn't you hear what they said? It's impossible!' Gustav's voice was a bit too shrill, and he went on in a more muted tone: 'We can't do it, Vivi. We'll have to wait until morning. Maybe by then the worst of the storm will be over, and we can make the crossing.'

'I wouldn't count on it,' said Harald. 'The weather forecast says that the storm is going to last until Sunday. So I suppose we'll just have to sit tight and wait.'

'But I can't stay here for two days. Not with a . . . corpse!' cried Vivi. Everyone was now looking at her.

'So what do you suggest we do? Skate across the ice to Fjällbacka?' Harald yelled.

Gustav sprang to his feet and put his arm around his wife.

'I won't have you speaking to Vivi in that tone of voice. Can't you see that she's in shock? We're all in shock.'

Harald merely snorted. Instead of replying, he poured himself a generous amount of cognac.

A faint voice now piped up from the chair closest to the window.

'How can all of you keep on arguing like this? Nobody has said a word about the fact that Grandpa is dead. He's gone! Don't you understand that? But none of you care. The only thing that matters to you is to keep on with your damn bickering. About such petty things! And about money! Grandpa was ashamed of all of you, and I can understand why.' Matte held back a sob as he wiped his eyes on the sleeve of his shirt.

'Listen to that,' sneered Bernard. He was lounging at one end of the sofa, twirling his cognac glass in his hand. 'Always Grandpa's favourite. Always ready to sit like a lapdog and listen to the old man's endless stories. You even pretended to be interested in that drivel about the Sherlock Holmes club. And yet you never hesitated to take his money.'

'Bernard . . .' pleaded Lisette, but her cousin paid no attention.

'He gave you that flat in the city when you started at the university. What was it worth? Three million? Four?'

'I never asked for anything!' retorted Matte, glaring at Bernard. 'Unlike the rest of you, I wasn't constantly begging him for money. The flat belonged to Grandpa, and I was allowed to live there while I studied, but as soon as I graduated, I would have to make it on my own. That was the agreement. And I didn't want it any other way. Grandpa knew that.'

Again he used his shirtsleeve to dry his tears.

Then he turned to look out of the window, clearly embarrassed that they'd seen him crying.

'Matte, we know how close you were to Grandpa. And all of us are sad. We're just a little . . . shocked . . . as Uncle Gustav said.' Britten perched on the armrest of Matte's chair and gently stroked his arm. He didn't push her away, but he kept his gaze fixed on the winter darkness.

'Well, maybe we should all turn in for the night,' said Harald, standing up. 'Before we say anything that we'll regret tomorrow.'

The others murmured their agreement, and the library quickly emptied. Only Vivi stayed behind.

'Our room is upstairs,' said Lisette as she took Martin's arm. 'Why don't you fetch your bag? I've already put mine in the room.'

He did as she said and then followed her up the stairs.

Even though the beds were marvellously comfortable, Martin lay awake for a long time, listening to Lisette breathing next to him. Outside, the blizzard raged, worse than ever. He wondered what the morning would bring.

It was a habit she'd had ever since childhood. Whenever she was nervous, she would play with the pearl necklace that had been a gift from her mother. And she'd certainly resorted to that nervous habit many times over the years. 'Viveca is very highly-strung,' she'd heard her mother say so often when she was growing up, until in the end it had become a self-fulfilling prophecy. At first she'd thought it was merely something the grown-ups said to explain the normal emotional outbursts of a child, and later a teenager. But gradually the statement had settled over her like a dingy veil. People treated her as if she had delicate nerves, and she found it simpler to live up to their expectations. By now she was afraid of everything. In addition to normal fears – spiders and snakes and the greenhouse effect and the proliferation of nuclear weapons – she was frightened by more subtle and ordinary things: the look someone gave her when they met, hidden meanings in what they said to her, unintentional insults and unanticipated attacks. Eventually, the whole world had become a threatening place, and she caught herself constantly playing with her necklace. But now it was gone. Hundreds of tiny pearls had scattered across the floor in the dining room. Kerstin had tried to console her, saying that she would gather up every one of them and have them restrung for a new necklace. And no doubt she would. But it wouldn't be the same. Something new could not become something old. Something that had been destroyed could never be whole again.

For a moment Vivi pictured in her mind Ruben's accusatory eyes. That expression she thought she always saw whenever he looked at her. Reproachful and filled with contempt for her weakness.

Oh, how she wished that she'd had just

one-hundredth of the strength that seemed to radiate from him. Not to mention that she wished Gustav had inherited at least a small part of his father's self-confidence. But together she and Gustav seemed even weaker than they did individually. If they hadn't joined forces against the threat that Ruben represented, which had held them together like glue all these years, Vivi knew they never would have survived. With a vacant expression she stared at the smouldering fire as she sensed disaster approaching like a speeding train. Old secrets had begun to stir, like a monster lurking below the surface.

The next day the storm was still raging. Börje and Kerstin had made a valiant attempt to clear a path at the front entrance, but the snowfall was so heavy that by now the drifts reached almost to the window ledges on the ground floor. If the storm continued like this for another twenty-four hours, they would soon be completely snowed in.

It was a subdued group that appeared for breakfast. Everyone found it unnerving to sit down at the same table where they'd all gathered the night before. Yet no one had offered any protests when their hosts asked if it would be all right to serve breakfast in the dining room. Once again there was an abundance of food. Boiled eggs, three kinds of cheese, ham, salami, bacon and bread fresh from the oven. But most of the family members hardly touched their food. Only Harald and Bernard ate heartily. Apparently they weren't going to let a murder ruin their appetite.

'Did you sleep well?' Britten asked everyone in an attempt to start a conversation, but aside from a few murmurs no one replied.

'Such comfortable beds,' she told Kerstin, who was walking around the table to serve the coffee.

Kerstin nodded and smiled. 'I hope you weren't cold. Let me know if you are, and I'll bring you some extra blankets.'

'No, it was fine. Perfect.' Britten looked around to see if anyone else would care to comment, but they were all staring down at their plates.

Martin couldn't bear the oppressive mood a second longer. He said brusquely, 'I'd like to continue with the interviews as soon as you've finished breakfast. Gustav, could you join me in the office in . . .' Martin glanced at his watch. 'Let's say ten minutes?'

'Certainly,' said Gustav. He and Vivi exchanged a glance that was difficult to interpret. 'Of course. I'll be there in ten minutes. So I'm next in line, is that right?' He uttered a brief laugh that bordered on falsetto. No one else laughed.

'Thanks. That would be great,' Martin said as he stood up. In truth there was nothing he had to prepare that required an extra ten minutes, but he wanted to retreat to the peace and quiet of the office to gather his thoughts.

Precisely ten minutes later Gustav Liljecrona entered the room. Once again Martin was struck by how different the two brothers were. Harald was a tall, broad-shouldered, and loud man with a bushy mane of hair. His younger brother was short and wiry with sloping shoulders. And whatever hair he'd once had was now a distant memory.

'So, here I am,' Gustav said as he sat down. Martin's response was to launch into his first question.

'How would you describe your relationship with your father?'

Gustav flinched and seemed to have a hard time deciding where to look. Finally he fixed his eyes on the desk as he stammered: 'Well, er, um. What should I say? It was like most father–son relationships. In other words, occasionally it could get a bit complicated.' He laughed nervously.

'A bit complicated?' Martin paged through his notes to find what he'd written about his interview with Harald. Then he went on. 'From what I understand, both you and your brother had a very complicated relationship with Ruben. But the same might be said of the interaction between you and Harald. It seems to be rather problematic.'

Gustav gave another nervous laugh. He still hadn't looked Martin in the eye. He kept his gaze steadfastly fixed on the desk.

'It's not always easy being a member of this family. To say that Father had high expectations would be an understatement.'

'I've heard that his intention in putting you and your brother in management positions at the family business was to bring you closer together. Is that right?'

Gustav's only reply was a disdainful snort.

'From what I can gather, things didn't work out too well,' Martin persisted.

'No, they didn't.' Gustav didn't seem particularly keen on discussing the topic, but that didn't stop Martin.

'I'm thinking about what your father said at the dinner table. About the company. What was he referring to?'

Now Gustav seemed genuinely uncomfortable as he shifted position on his chair. 'I have no idea,' he said after a moment. It was the same answer that his brother had given. Martin didn't believe either of them.

'But he must have had something specific in mind. Besides, the last thing he did was more or less vow to disinherit all of you. That's a pretty drastic step to take.'

'It was nothing but hot air,' said Gustav, fidgeting with the hem of his jacket. 'He's issued that same threat before. It was a way for him to show who was in charge, and it made him feel that he still had some power. But he didn't mean anything by it.'

'That wasn't my impression,' said Martin.

'But you don't know the family very well,' snapped Gustav, tugging even harder at his jacket. He looked uneasy.

Martin continued to question Gustav for another

half hour, but got nothing useful out of him. He continued to maintain that no one in the family would dream of killing Ruben. And no, he hadn't noticed anything suspicious during the course of the day or evening. No, he didn't understand what his father was referring to in the statements he'd made at dinner.

Eventually a cautious knock on the door interrupted the interview. It was Kerstin.

'I'm sorry to disturb you. I just wanted to say that we're serving coffee in the library, so when you're done here . . .'

Martin sighed. 'We may as well stop now. But we'll continue our talk later.' He hadn't intended it to sound like a threat, but Gustav gave a start. Then he stood up and hurried out of the office.

Martin was feeling more and more frustrated. He began to wonder if he was up to the job. Once again he wished that Patrik Hedström were here to advise him. But he wasn't. So there was nothing for it but to take charge and do the best he could. As soon as they were able to make contact with civilization again, he'd summon the backup that he needed. If he could only stand his ground until then, everything would be fine.

Martin could hear raised voices as he walked down the corridor towards the library. When he entered the room he saw Gustav and Harald. Both men were red in the face, and saliva was flying as they shouted at each other.

'You're always so conceited! You think you're better at everything!' yelled Gustav, shaking his fist at his brother.

'If I'm conceited, it's because I *am* better at everything than you are! Name one thing you've ever succeeded at – go on, name one thing!'

The flush on Harald's face made Martin worry that the man might be on the verge of a heart attack. Apparently Britten had the same thought because she was standing behind her husband, trying to calm him down by pulling on his arm and pleading with him to stop.

'As if you've had so much success yourself! I heard why those American suppliers backed out last spring. They considered you to be incompetent and unreliable – you even managed to insult their CEO. So thanks to you we lost a contract that could have generated up to ten per cent of next year's sales!'

Harald made a lunge for Gustav, who hastily jumped away. Britten tugged even harder at her husband's arm, trying to hold him back.

'Harald, please. Stop this. It's so unnecessary. You're brothers, after all. And think about your blood pressure . . .' But her husband refused to listen to her.

'Well, at least I'm not an embezzler,' Harald snarled. He turned to Martin. 'You didn't know about that, did you? My dear brother has been withdrawing money from the company accounts for over a year. More than five million kronor in total. The auditors just found out about it, and that

40

was probably what Father was referring to at dinner. So if you're looking for a motive, there it is – five million kronor.'

Harald pointed triumphantly at Gustav, whose face had turned so white that it seemed almost transparent.

'Ha! What do you have to say for yourself now?' Harald shook off Britten's hand and folded his arms. He looked like the proverbial cat who'd swallowed a very plump canary.

'It was . . . it was a loan,' stammered Gustav. 'I was going to pay the money back. On my word of honour. Every single öre. I only borrowed it because . . . I . . .' He turned to look at Vivi who, like Britten, was standing beside her husband. She was staring at him wide-eyed.

'Gustav?' Again Vivi raised her hand to her throat. 'What . . . what is Harald talking about? Five million kronor? Gustav?'

With a look of despair he stretched out a hand to his wife, who quickly took a step back to avoid his touch.

'Sweetheart . . . I . . .' Gustav turned towards the window, as if trying to find a way out, but the blizzard had not let up in the slightest, and it had effectively cut off all escape routes. Then he sank into a chair and buried his face in his hands. In utter silence the others stared at him. Vivi in disbelief, Harald with a triumphant expression, Bernard with obvious glee, and Britten with a certain amount of sympathy.

'What did you do with the money?' Vivi was the first to break the silence, her voice quavering. When she received no reply, she repeated her question. 'Gustav, what did you do with the money?'

First they heard a deep sigh, then came his answer, the words barely intelligible.

'I . . . gambled it all away.'

Vivi inhaled sharply. Bernard laughed. Martin saw Miranda give him a sharp jab in the side as she hissed: 'Stop that!'

'You . . . gambled the money away?' Vivi shook her head and seemed unable to comprehend what she'd heard. 'Gambled on what?'

Still with his face buried in his hands, Gustav muttered: 'Horses, Internet poker games – you name it. Anything that would give me that adrenalin rush. And in the beginning I won. I won big time. But then I started losing. I thought that if I kept going for a little while, I'd win it all back. Then I could return the money to the company.'

'What a bloody loser you are,' said Harald with disgust.

Gustav abruptly raised his head and glared at his brother with hatred.

'I don't see why you're so proud of yourself. You've been a total failure as CEO, and Father was ready to sack you. And you know it. What would you have done then? No management job, no money from Father, nothing. You've taken advantage of Father's generosity all your life, and you never had to make it on your own. So if we're going to talk about motive, that's a strong motive too!' Gustav turned to look at Martin as he uttered this last remark. Then he got up and stormed out of the library.

For a moment the silence almost echoed in the room, until Bernard said cheerfully, 'Well, the entertainment seems to be over. How about some coffee?'

It never ceased to amaze him how self-destructive they were. To think that his father had actually been enterprising enough to embezzle five million kronor – and then gamble all the money away! Bernard could scarcely believe it. He chuckled to himself as he took a cinnamon bun. He supposed he ought to feel sorry for the old man, but he'd never had much time for empathy. It was a constant marvel to him that someone as decisive and strong as he was could have come from such pitiful parents. There must be some truth in the theory of environment versus genetics.

He sat down at a table where his sister was sitting alone, listlessly stirring her coffee.

'Don't you want anything sweet with your coffee?' he asked, pointing behind him to the platter that was piled high with baked goods.

'No. I'm on a diet,' she told him in a tone of voice that indicated this was a standard phrase of hers.

'Suit yourself.' Bernard took a big bite of a cinnamon bun.

'I don't understand how you can eat so many pastries and never get fat,' said Miranda, looking at him with disgust.

'Good genes,' he said, grinning as he patted his flat stomach.

'I guess you won the lottery in that respect,' grumbled Miranda. 'You got Mum and Dad's good genes, while I got . . . Who the hell knows?' And she laughed.

'That's probably the only good thing I got from them,' he said with a wry smile.

'I know.' Miranda sighed. It was not the first time they had discussed this topic and concluded that neither of them had much in common with their parents.

'So what do you think about all this?' Bernard asked, taking another bite of the bun.

'All this? Hmm . . .' said Miranda.

'Are you thinking the same thing I am?' whispered Bernard.

'That maybe he already changed his will?' whispered Miranda in reply. 'Yes, the thought did occur to me.'

'Even so, there's no reason to panic. We can always contest the will. I'm certain we can find witnesses who will testify that the old man was not in his right mind at the end.'

'Maybe,' said Miranda, looking sceptical. She was still aimlessly stirring her coffee, but now she stopped. 'Who do you think killed him?' she whispered, glancing around the room.

'I have no idea,' said Bernard. 'Absolutely no idea.' He stuffed the last bite of cinnamon bun in his mouth.

Martin felt a numbing fatigue come over him, the result of consuming far too many biscuits and pastries. He knew he should search Ruben's room to see if he could find anything that might propel the investigation forward, but first he decided to lie down and rest for a while. He needed a break so he could think everything through. To his annoyance, Lisette accompanied him up to their room. Instead of having some peace and quiet, he found himself lying on the bed next to her, listening to her babble.

'I think it's terrible that Uncle Gustav embezzled money from Grandpa's company. And yet he has the gall to say such awful things about my father . . . How could anyone suggest that . . . that my father would . . . Oh, poor Pappa. You know, I've never been very fond of Uncle Gustav and Aunt Vivi. I have to admit that.'

Martin sighed. In the early days he had found Lisette and her bubbly chatter so charming, but now, as if with the speed of lightning, she had ceased to be attractive to him. He knew now that their relationship had been a summer love affair that should have gone no further. Why did he always choose the wrong girlfriends? Sometimes he wondered if he'd ever find anyone to share his life. At the moment, it seemed highly unlikely. On the other hand, he wasn't exactly ancient, so he still had time. But first he needed to untangle himself from this terrible blunder that he'd made.

'I simply can't understand how Gustav could be Bernard's father. My cousin is such a handsome and stylish guy,' Lisette was saying. 'Vivi was pretty when she was younger. I've seen pictures of her. So maybe that's where he gets his good looks. And Miranda is beautiful. Don't you think so, Martin?'

From Lisette's tone of voice Martin sensed that he was stepping into a minefield, and the best policy would be to ignore the question entirely. So he feigned a snore and hoped that Lisette would be fooled into thinking that he'd dozed off. Thank God, it must have worked, because she didn't repeat the question.

A moment later he fell asleep for real.

Martin sat up with a jolt and quickly realized that he'd slept for over an hour. He cursed as he tossed aside the blanket. The other side of the bed was empty and cold, so Lisette must have left quite a while ago. Annoyed, he ran his hand through his tousled hair and stepped out into the corridor. Out of the corner of his eye he glimpsed two shadows hurriedly disappearing at the sound of his door opening. He dashed after them, but when he reached the stairs, they were gone. He wondered who had been so eager to avoid him, and why.

Still groggy, Martin went downstairs. Hearing voices in the library, he headed in that direction.

The storm didn't seem to have diminished. If anything, it was worse. The strain of being trapped indoors under these circumstances was evident in the pallid faces and tense expressions of the assembled family members. Martin glanced around the room suspiciously, hoping to spot the two people who'd run away from him upstairs, but no one looked particularly nervous or out of breath.

'So, the sleeper awakes,' bellowed Harald. 'Nice to see how my tax money is put to use. The officer in charge lies in bed snoring while there's a murderer on the loose.' He chuckled as Britten gave him a jab in the side. Apparently she found his humour in poor taste.

'I'd like to continue with the interviews.' Martin could hear how irritable he sounded, so he added in a calmer tone: 'Bernard, would you mind . . .'

Bernard didn't deign to answer. He merely raised one eyebrow, nonchalantly set down his glass, and then followed Martin out of the room.

'Were you upstairs a moment ago?' Martin asked, trying to sound casual while intently studying the man seated on the other side of the desk.

'Upstairs? No, I was in the library. You saw me there, didn't you?' replied Bernard, crossing his legs in that annoying way of his.

Martin wasn't sure that he believed him, but he persisted, 'Did you see anyone else come down the stairs a few minutes ago?'

'Hmm . . . No. Everybody was in the library. I thought this interview was supposed to be about what happened last night. About who killed dear Grandpa Ruben, whose body is now resting in the cold-storage room.'

'Yes, let's talk about last night. Your grandfather certainly had harsh words for you at the dinner table. What was he referring to? Who are the "sources" that he mentioned, and what did they have to say about the business that you're involved in?'

Bernard plucked a few invisible pieces of lint from his immaculately pressed trousers. Then he looked Martin in the eye, a smile tugging at the corner of his lips. It seemed to Martin that everything about this man radiated contempt, a sense of superiority towards everyone else.

'As I'm sure you heard me say at dinner, I have no idea what Grandpa was talking about. My company is flourishing. In fact, we've recently gone public, and as far as Grandpa's sources are concerned . . . well, all I can say is the old man wasn't in the game any more. His so-called sources are a bunch of has-beens. They've ceased to be players, so they spend their time spreading malicious rumours.'

'I didn't get the impression that your grandfather was a has-been. On the contrary.'

Bernard snorted. He plucked away more invisible lint before replying.

'Grandpa Ruben put my father and Harald in two of the most important positions in his company. Does that strike you as a sound and intelligent commercial decision?'

Martin could see what he meant. Maybe it was

true that the old man had no longer been fully cognizant of what he was doing.

'There seems to have been a pattern among members of the Liljecrona family of asking Ruben for various . . . infusions of cash. Did you make use of the family assets in the same way?'

'What if I did? We were going to inherit his money sooner or later. It was better for the old man to help us out while he was still alive. Then he could hear us thank him for his generosity. And share in our success . . .'

'How much?' asked Martin coldly.

'How much what?' Bernard pretended not to understand the question.

'How much did you get Ruben to invest in your company?'

For a moment Bernard seemed to lose his composure. He paused before replying:

'Twenty million.'

'Twenty million?' repeated Martin in disbelief. The sum made him dizzy.

'He was going to get it all back, and with interest. As soon as the IPO went through.'

'Then what was the problem he mentioned last night? It sounded as though your grandfather had misgivings about his investment.'

'As I said before, I have no idea what he was talking about! The IPO will go through in a couple of weeks, and then he would have received his twenty million back, along with a whole sack of money in interest!' Bernard's unflappable composure seemed to be showing a few cracks. He ran his hand over his slicked-back hair.

'So if I ask the fraud squad to check out your company when we get back to civilization, they're not going to find anything amiss?'

Again Bernard ran his hand over his gelled hair. Martin felt great satisfaction when he noticed him shift his glance away for a moment.

'How many times do I have to say it? I have no idea what Grandpa was talking about,' he muttered through clenched teeth.

'So you maintain that you had no motive for killing him. What about the others? Is there anyone in the family who could have done it?'

Bernard was once again his usual smug self. And he said more or less what his sister had said. 'Do you really expect me to answer that question?'

'Okay, let's stop there for the time being,' said Martin, realizing that he wasn't going to make any more headway with Bernard. 'Could you ask Mattias to join me here in the office?'

'No one calls him Mattias. Just Matte. But I'll pass on your message to my dear cousin.'

With that Bernard got up and sauntered out of the room. Martin watched with annoyance. There was something about the man that made his hackles rise.

'You wanted to see me?'

Matte paused politely in the doorway. Martin noticed that his eyes were red-rimmed and realized that he'd shed more tears overnight.

'Yes, come in,' he said in a friendly tone of voice as he gestured towards the chair in front of the desk.

Matte obligingly sat down. 'What a terrible first meeting you've had with my family,' he said with a wan smile.

'You're right. It must be some kind of record,' said Martin with a laugh. Then his expression turned serious. 'How are you doing?'

Matte shook his head. 'I can't believe that Grandpa is gone . . . And that everyone seems so . . . indifferent.'

'I know what you mean,' said Martin. 'So far you're the only one I've seen cry over Ruben Liljecrona. I assume that the two of you must have been very close, you and your grandfather.'

'We had a ritual, Grandpa and I. Once a week, every Friday afternoon, I would call by his flat for tea. We talked about every subject under the sun. Grandpa was one of the cleverest, most widely read, and most broad-minded people I've ever met. It was a privilege to have him in my life.'

'It doesn't appear that the rest of the family shared your opinion.'

Matte snorted. 'The others just got dollar signs in their eyes whenever they thought about Grandpa. Even my father. All they ever cared about was taking more and more money from him. Nobody was interested in getting to know him.'

'So the flat that Bernard mentioned . . .'

Matte sighed wearily. 'Grandpa and I had an

51

agreement. I was allowed to live in a flat that he owned while I was studying at the university. He never signed the property over to me. I leased it from him, that's all.'

Martin paused before saying in a low voice, 'Do you have any idea who might have done this?'

A few seconds passed before Matte reacted. Then he merely shook his head and said, 'No. I have no idea.'

Martin had the feeling that Matte wanted to say more, so he persisted:

'Are you sure? Do you have any suspicions about who might have wanted to kill your grandfather?'

'No. None,' replied Matte in a firmer voice. 'It's true that everyone took advantage of him, but to go from that to murder . . . No, I can't imagine anyone doing that.'

Martin gave him a searching glance before concluding, 'In that case, I have no more questions at the moment.'

'No more questions?' said Matte in surprise. 'But there must be other things that—'

'I do have a number of things I plan to ask all of you in the hope of getting to the bottom of this matter. But right now I'm primarily interested in forming a general picture of how things stood. I'll get to back to you later.'

Matte stood up but didn't immediately leave the office. He paused in the doorway, as if he wanted to say something else. Martin waited, but in the end Matte simply turned around and left.

Martin wondered what other questions he should have asked.

Matte felt his legs shaking as he exited the office. There was something in the red-haired police officer's expression that left him feeling stripped naked. As if he'd been revealed for the fraud that he was. The familiar sense of panic began churning in the pit of his stomach. It started as a tiny rumbling, but he knew that it would only grow in strength if he didn't stop it. When he was younger, he'd had no choice but to allow the wave of panic to surge through him, faster and faster until it practically suffocated him. Now, he'd learned how to handle it. He had the tools, as the psychologist would have told him. So he took a few more steps over to the wall and leaned his back against it as he slowly sank to the floor in a seated position. He rested his forehead on his knees and closed his eyes. The important thing was to focus on the point in the middle of the darkness. He could make the point grow, and then it would force him to get his breathing under control. In and out. In and out. One calm breath after another. One breath at a time until his pulse no longer threatened to run away with him. The darkness behind his eyelids soothed him. And today he had company in that darkness. Deep inside that point that was growing and growing he saw his grandfather. Ruben was waving to him. Giving him a wink. Showing him that everything was okay. Everything was as it should be.

A few minutes later, Matte got up. For the time being, the attack was over.

'When do you suppose we'll be able to get out of here?' Vivi's lower lip quivered.

'As I've already told you, not until the storm dies down.' Martin couldn't suppress the impatience in his voice. How hard could it be to understand? It was impossible to cross the water to the mainland at the moment. Then he instantly felt guilty. The woman sitting in front of him looked as if she were on the verge of falling apart, without him making matters worse by being rude.

'It's bound to clear up soon,' he said kindly, handing her a tissue which she gratefully accepted.

Then he went on: 'I understand that this must be a terrible strain for you. For all of you.'

'Yes, it is,' sobbed Vivi as she wiped her eyes with the tissue. 'It's starting to feel like too much for me, this whole situation. I have delicate nerves, you see.'

Martin nodded sympathetically. 'I promise to proceed as gently as possible. But it's important that we find out who did this.'

'Yes, yes, of course,' said Vivi and she blotted her eyes. The tissue was streaked with mascara.

'How much did you know about your husband's . . .' Martin searched for the right word. '. . . activities?'

Vivi began crying even harder, pressing the tissue

to her eyes. Her other hand fumbled nervously at her throat.

'Nothing. Nothing at all. To think that he could . . .' Her voice broke and she seemed to give up the battle to save her make-up. Two streaks of mascara formed on her cheeks.

'No, I had absolutely no idea.' She crushed the tissue in her hands, which now rested on her lap. Martin subjected her to a penetrating look, but he was inclined to believe her. He dropped that line of questioning and moved on to another topic.

'How was your relationship with Ruben?'

Vivi stopped crying, then said, 'We . . . well, I wouldn't say that we had much of a relationship with him. Ruben never thought very highly of me. In fact, he more or less ignored me. Besides, he always made me nervous.'

'Nervous?' said Martin.

'Yes. He had such an air of authority. And Gustav was always so stressed when they were together, so eager to please his father. I suppose his feelings got transmitted to me, so . . . Yes, I think nervous is the correct word.'

'Do you have any theories as to who might have had reason to kill your father-in-law?'

Again Vivi's hand reached for her throat. 'No, no. I can't imagine that anyone would do something like that. It's unthinkable. Utterly unthinkable!'

'And yet someone did murder him,' said Martin, cocking his head to one side.

Vivi merely shifted uneasily in her seat without replying. Either she couldn't or wouldn't answer the question.

Martin was about to continue when a noise made both of them turn to look at the door. Agitated voices and the sound of crashing furniture could be heard from the library. Martin jumped to his feet. Seconds later he entered the room to see Matte and Bernard in a stand-off, and apparently Matte had gained the upper hand. He had Bernard backed up against the wall, and was holding his cousin's shirt in an iron grip as he shouted at him. Saliva flew, but Bernard didn't dare reach up to wipe it off his face.

'Shut the fuck up, you bastard! Do you hear me? Shut up!' Matte's face was white with rage, and with each word, he pressed Bernard harder against the wall. They were standing right next to the Christmas tree, which had started to sway ominously.

'Bernard didn't mean . . .' Gustav looked bewildered as he stared at his son and nephew.

'Gustav, what's going on?' cried Vivi as she came rushing into the library behind Martin.

'Your son was accusing my son.' Britten's voice was as cold as ice as she turned to look at her sister-in-law. Then she turned back to Matte and began pleading in a much gentler tone:

'Matte, please, stop this. Let Bernard go. Don't pay any attention to what he says. He's an idiot. You know that.'

'What the hell are you saying about my son?' Gustav roared at Britten.

'You heard what I said, Gustav. It's no secret that your son is a first-class idiot!'

'I can't believe you'd say such a thing when your own son is a mental wreck! If it weren't for Ruben, he'd still be locked up in that place. And obviously that's where he belongs.'

Gustav and Britten were glaring at each other like two combatants. Standing next to them, Matte continued to hold Bernard in a firm grip as if oblivious to what was going on around him. The rest of the Liljecrona family seemed to be frozen in place.

Martin realized that he had to take action. In his most authoritative voice, he shouted: 'Everybody calm down!' Then he strode over to Matte and pulled him away from Bernard. It was surprisingly easy. All the air seemed to seep out of Matte the moment Martin took his arm, and he collapsed onto the nearest armchair.

Bernard rubbed his hand over his chest. The front of his shirt was severely wrinkled, and he was undoubtedly going to have bruises on his neck. Since Martin hadn't heard what prompted the quarrel, he didn't know whether Bernard had deserved such treatment or not.

'All right now. Everybody calm down,' Martin repeated.

'He should be locked up! What a fucking lunatic!' snapped Bernard, glaring at Matte. But Lisette's brother was no longer paying attention to him. He sat in the chair, hunched forward, with his head in his hands and his eyes staring into space.

Britten went over and knelt down next to his chair. Gently she stroked Matte's back as she spoke to him quietly, trying to soothe him.

'My God, that man has never been right in the head!' declared Bernard as he straightened his tie.

'Take it easy,' said Gustav, motioning for his son to move further away from Matte. Bernard complied but continued to stare angrily at his cousin.

'I know that you're all under a great deal of pressure,' said Martin, looking around the room, 'but we need to try and make the best of the situation. I'm sure that we'll be able to reach the mainland very soon, but until then I suggest that everyone remain calm.' He stared pointedly at the two men who had been fighting before repeating what he'd already said. 'Everybody needs to stay calm. Okay?'

Bernard reluctantly nodded agreement, but Matte appeared not to have heard. He abruptly stood up and dashed out of the library, heading upstairs to his room. Britten was about to run after him, but Harald put his hand on her arm to stop her.

'Let him go. He needs to be alone.'

'It's just so typical!' Lisette was standing at the other end of the room. 'Matte always has to make a scene.'

'Lisette, shouldn't you be defending your

brother? You heard what your dear cousin said to him. It's only natural he would react the way he did.' Britten gave her daughter a furious look.

'Well, Bernard was right. He's a total nutcase.' Lisette's voice rose shrilly, and Martin thought to himself that she was becoming less and less attractive by the minute.

'Lisette!' cried Britten, halting any further comment from her daughter.

Martin took the opportunity to repeat his admonition, this time directing the words at his girlfriend.

'As I said, everybody needs to calm down. All this bickering isn't helping. We have to try to get through the hours until we're able to make contact with the mainland.'

The look that Lisette gave him revealed that she wasn't going to be particularly pleasant to be around. Not that it mattered. Once they got out of here, he had no intention of seeing her again.

Martin turned his back on all of them and went to the kitchen to get some coffee. Right now he was sick and tired of the whole Liljecrona family.

Lisette watched, seething, as Martin left the room. How dare he reprimand her like that! And her mother too! But both of her parents had always pampered Matte. Showering him with attention – at Lisette's expense. 'You're managing so well on your own. We need to give Matte a little help . . .' So Matte came first with them. And when, during his first year at university, all his fears and insecurities got too much for him and he fell apart completely, she might as well have been invisible. All they could talk about was 'poor Matte', who couldn't handle the pressure of studying and needed time to 'rest'. Even Grandpa Ruben had been worried. Matte had been his favourite from the start. It was all so unfair.

Lisette exchanged glances with Bernard across the room. He was the only one who understood. They'd spent many evenings together, drinking wine as they both harped on the faults of their parents. On a few occasions they'd ended up in bed together. But that was not something they ever mentioned; they were first cousins, after all. Which was a shame, because Lisette had always thought they were made for each other. He was a real man, to his very fingertips. Unlike Martin, who had turned out to be incredibly . . . insipid. Not that she could ever have been happy living on a policeman's salary. It was laughable – she received more in pocket money from her father.

She couldn't help smiling to herself as she thought about her assignation with Bernard earlier. Martin had almost caught the pair of them, but they had managed to sneak away in the nick of time.

'Lisette, I wish you could be more considerate of Matte.'

Britten had suddenly appeared at her side, and

Lisette gave a start at the touch of her mother's hand.

'Matte, Matte, Matte – I can't stand to hear another word about him. Why do you always have to defend him? Didn't you see how he attacked poor Bernard?'

'*Poor Bernard*,' snorted Britten. 'I wish you'd be more objective when it comes to your cousin. Didn't you hear what he said to Matte? Of course I don't condone the way Matte attacked him. Violence never solves anything. But I do understand why he reacted the way he did. What Bernard said was so inappropriate.'

'Inappropriate! Do you think it was more appropriate for Matte to try and strangle Bernard?' Lisette's voice rose even higher, and everyone turned to look at her and Britten. Harald cast an apologetic glance around as he hurried over to his wife and daughter.

'Shh . . . Let's stop all this quarrelling. Get a hold of yourselves,' he pleaded. Lisette enjoyed seeing her father look so uncomfortable. He was a cowardly man who would go to any lengths to avoid conflict. Britten had been left to handle any serious issues with the children while Harald had conveniently kept out of the way. Even now his eyes were nervously shifting about. Lisette looked at him with contempt, the same contempt she felt for the entire family. Her only consolation had been the prospect of inheriting Grandpa Ruben's money and giving them all the finger. Then she could fulfil her dream to live on the Riviera and enjoy every day as if there were no tomorrow. Forget about all the studying and simply . . . live!

She gave Harald and Britten a cold glare. Then she turned on her heel and left the room with only one thought in her head: she had to get out of here. And soon.

Börje and Kerstin were busy preparing lunch when Martin walked in.

'Would you mind if I had some coffee?' he asked, nodding towards the coffee maker on the worktop.

'Help yourself,' said Kerstin. She was slicing a loaf of rye bread.

Martin poured himself a cup. With his back to the doorway, he peered out of the window. The storm showed no sign of letting up.

'It's certainly looking lively out there,' said Börje. He was taking drinks out of the fridge, the bottles clinking.

'You can say that again.' Martin took a sip of his coffee but it almost burned his lips. He'd have to wait for it to cool off a bit.

'So . . .' Kerstin had turned to face Martin but seemed reluctant to go on. 'So . . . We were wondering if you could possibly fetch the roast beef. It needs to thaw out before we can make dinner.'

At first Martin couldn't understand why they wanted him to take care of this household chore. Then he realized it was because Ruben's body was in the cold-storage room.

He set down his coffee cup and said, 'Of course. No problem.'

Kerstin and Börje both looked relieved.

In spite of his cheerful tone of voice, Martin hesitated before pressing down the handle. Because he was a police officer, the couple undoubtedly assumed that he was accustomed to seeing corpses. And that may have been the case if he'd been part of an inner-city police district. But thus far in his career he had seen only two dead bodies – one was the victim of a car accident north of Tanumshede, the other a drunken tourist who had drowned.

He stepped inside the cold-storage room. And there lay Ruben. Martin was surprised that the sight didn't make him feel sick. Somehow the space seemed quite peaceful.

Ruben lay on his back on the table where they'd placed him the night before. It was strange that less than twenty-four hours had passed since that dramatic dinner. The claustrophobic atmosphere in the hotel made it seem that they'd all been shut inside for weeks, months, an eternity.

Martin cautiously walked past the table towards the freezer. Out of the corner of his eye he thought he saw something move, but then realized he was imagining things. Ruben's body was perfectly motionless.

The lid of the freezer was stuck, so he had to yank on it with all his might. A cold gust swept over him and he took a step back. The roast beef was lying on top, neatly labelled with a woman's handwriting. The large packet was so cold that it burned his hands. Martin hurried past Ruben. When the door closed behind him, he felt a great sense of relief, even though he hadn't found it unpleasant to be inside with the dead man.

'How did it go?' asked Kerstin. Judging by her tone of voice, you'd have thought he'd skied all the way to the North Pole instead of simply fetching a roast from the freezer.

'Fine,' said Martin, gratefully putting down the ice-cold packet. He rubbed his hands to get the circulation moving and then reached for his coffee cup, which now felt pleasantly warm.

'What do you think about this situation? Have you made any progress?' asked Börje, nodding towards the cold-storage room.

Martin felt his heart sink. He could only tell them the truth.

'No, I can't say that I have. No one saw anything. No one knows anything. And there seems to be no motive. Yet they're constantly bickering, like a bunch of cats and dogs.'

Börje chuckled. 'I heard this was going to be your first encounter with them. That you were invited here to meet the family. What a hell of an introduction!'

Kerstin jabbed her elbow into her husband's side. 'Börje, what a thing to say!'

Martin laughed. 'That's okay. You're absolutely right. It's been hell!'

All three laughed, and Martin felt the pressure in his chest ease.

Hatred continued to pump through his body. He'd been forced to escape, otherwise the hatred would have taken over, conquered him, and made him do things that he would regret. Matte rhythmically clenched and unclenched his fists as he sat in his room with his back to the door. Only with the door closed and locked could he feel secure. He never felt safe unless he was alone. Other people represented a danger, a threat. They might be full of good intentions, or even love, but they were still basically dangerous and deceitful. The only person he'd ever felt safe with was his grandfather. In Ruben's company, Matte had been able to relax and be himself. He could tell the old man all the thoughts that kept racing through his mind, moving every which way, constantly searching for cracks in the wall. Looking for somewhere to hide. Grandpa had understood. He'd never questioned him. Never yelled at him the way Pappa did, or cried the way Mamma did, or stared at him with that scornful expression that Lisette gave him. Grandpa had never taunted him as Bernard often did.

The others didn't know. They didn't understand why he hated Bernard with all his heart. Matte had tried to restrain himself, tried to sweep his memories under the rug. Tried to behave properly. The way they wanted him to do. But his memories were impossible to escape. They surfaced as soon as he let down his guard. He and Bernard had attended the same school. They weren't in the same class, but only a few years apart. And Bernard had tormented him the whole time. He'd taken the lead and the other pupils had followed his example, pummelling Matte with taunts and punches, laughing at him, ridiculing him. Always there. Always smiling. Always looking for new ways to hurt him. The situation improved as they got older. They hadn't attended the same secondary school, and by that time Bernard had in any case grown tired of devising new outlets for his malicious energy. But the antagonism would reappear whenever they happened to meet. And that smile. Bernard had seen through Matte; he knew exactly which buttons to press in order to crush him.

It was the only thing that Matte had never told Grandpa. He knew that on some level Ruben saw Bernard for the bully that he was, but not entirely. He still had hope that Bernard might change. And Matte hadn't wanted to take that hope away. That was why he'd never said a word when Ruben talked about Bernard. He'd held his tongue when his grandfather said things like: 'He'll make something of himself one day. You'll see. He just needs some time to play. But he's a good person at heart.' Matte could only look at Ruben in amazement and wonder, did he truly believe what he was saying? Didn't he see past the mask? The evil sneering behind Bernard's beautiful, perfect smile? Maybe,

maybe not. No matter what, Matte decided early on that he didn't want to be the one who robbed Grandpa Ruben of hope. With time, everything was bound to work out.

But now there was no more time left. Grandpa was dead. Matte's only friend in the world was gone. The one person he'd ever felt safe with. Gone. And Bernard's jeering smile provoked him. Signalling that Bernard was the one who had triumphed.

Suddenly a great crashing sound rattled all the windows. The snowstorm had brought thunder! At that moment Matte realized what he had to do. But first he needed to rest for a while. He lay down on the bed and closed his eyes. After only a few breaths, he fell asleep.

'Well, that's what I call drama.' Gustav Liljecrona and the rest of the family were sitting on the white sofa and matching armchairs. From the kitchen marvellous aromas came wafting into the library, and Gustav's stomach growled loudly.

'I'm looking forward to lunch,' he said with forced merriment as he took a sip of cognac, which had already begun to flow freely. On a weekend like this, all conventions had to be set aside.

No one replied to his attempt at small talk. Bernard rubbed his throat and muttered, 'God damn it, I'm probably going to have a huge fucking bruise. And how am I supposed to explain that at work? I leave to spend the weekend with my family and come back looking like somebody tried to strangle me.'

'Matte's always been unstable. I don't understand why they didn't realize that long ago. He's a serious danger to everyone.' Gustav shook his head as he swirled the cognac in his glass.

'Do you think that . . .?' Miranda hesitated but then went on. 'Do you think that Matte was the one who . . .' She couldn't make herself finish what she had planned to say, but she didn't need to. A glint appeared in everyone else's eyes.

'Of course!' said Bernard, now looking considerably happier. He sat up straight on the sofa and continued eagerly. 'My God. Of course it was Matte! He's always had something wrong with him, mentally. And you saw how he attacked me.'

'But . . . he and Ruben were so close,' said Vivi. Her objection was dismissed by Gustav, who also suddenly had a zealous look in his eye.

'Maybe that's why. It makes it even more plausible that Matte would have killed him. Who knows how he perceives things in that brain of his. Isn't it true that people are most often murdered by someone they know?'

Bernard and Gustav nodded at each other with satisfaction. Miranda still looked uncertain. She didn't seem convinced, even though she was the one who had first broached the idea.

'But . . .' she began, looking for support from her mother before she went on. 'But . . . what motive could he have?'

'Money, revenge, imagined offences. Who can tell?' snorted Bernard.

'I don't know,' said Miranda, plucking at a sofa cushion. 'I'm not sure . . .'

'But I am,' said Bernard, standing up. 'I'm going to have a talk with Lisette's policeman. He needs to have a clearer picture of how things stand. It wouldn't surprise me if he turns out to be rather interested in this particular theory.'

'But . . .' said Miranda again. She was about to say more, but Bernard was already on his way out the door.

She suddenly wished that she'd kept her mouth shut. She was actually quite fond of Matte. And he wasn't nearly as off balance as they made him out to be. Good Lord, practically everyone she knew had suffered some sort of nervous breakdown at one time or another. And taking Prozac or whatever drug had become so commonplace that nobody even raised an eyebrow any more. On the contrary. Plus it wasn't so strange that Matte had flown at Bernard. She loved her brother, but he could be incredibly aggressive. He had an unerring ability to sniff out people's weaknesses, and then he took a perverse pleasure in pressing their buttons.

'What will Harald and Britten say when they hear that Bernard has accused Matte of murdering Ruben?' asked Vivi anxiously as she fidgeted on the sofa.

'Who the hell cares what they say?' replied

Gustav, still swirling the cognac in his glass. 'Matte is clearly an unstable and aggressive individual. It's not much of a stretch to picture him as the most likely candidate.'

'But a murderer . . .' said Vivi, giving Miranda a pleading look.

'I have to agree with Mamma,' Miranda said, to her own surprise. It was rare for her to see eye to eye with Vivi, but for once they seemed to be on the same side. 'I know that I was the one who planted the seed, but . . . no. Matte as a cold-blooded killer? That doesn't feel right at all.'

'Women!' snorted Gustav, taking a gulp of the golden liquid before continuing. 'You're always so gullible. What do you think a murderer looks like? A crazy man with a big beard and lots of tattoos? Personally, I reckon Matte is more than capable of killing someone.' With a smug expression, he leaned back in his chair, apparently thinking he'd had the last word.

Miranda and Vivi exchanged a glance. Both sensed that this was not good. Not good at all.

'Did we make a mistake?' asked Britten quietly. She and Harald had retreated to the dining room to escape from the rest of the family for a while. Both Matte and Lisette had stormed upstairs to their rooms. Gustav and his family were in the library, no doubt gloating over all the commotion. And out of the corner of her eye Britten could see Martin Molin in the kitchen, talking to the hotel

70

owners. Harald was sitting across from her, his face such an ashen grey colour that she instantly grew concerned.

'Are you all right?' she said, placing her hand over Harald's. He smiled, but it was a strained smile.

'Don't worry about me.'

'You know that I can't help worrying.'

'Yes, I know.' Harald smiled again and then pulled his hand back so he could place it on top of hers. He meant the gesture to be reassuring, but it wasn't.

'I've made some fresh coffee. Help yourselves,' said Kerstin as she went over to the sideboard to set down a tray holding a thermos jug and cups. Then she returned to the kitchen.

'Would you like some?' Britten asked her husband as she stood up and moved towards the sideboard. Harald nodded, so she filled two cups. Black for herself, and milk with two lumps of sugar for Harald. She'd spent years trying to get him to stop putting sugar in his coffee, but in the end she'd realized that it was a battle she couldn't win.

'You didn't forget the sugar, did you?' asked Harald, giving his coffee a suspicious look.

Britten smiled. 'No, sweetheart. I didn't forget the sugar.' They knew each other so well.

She took a few sips of her coffee and then repeated her initial question. 'Did we make a mistake?'

'You mean with Matte?' Harald stirred his coffee to dissolve the sugar.

'With Matte and Lisette. She's right, you know. We've neglected her. Matte always got so much attention, whereas she was forever being told to be a good girl and help out. We left her to manage on her own. But she didn't – manage on her own, I mean. And she still can't.'

'What should we have done instead?' replied Harald wearily, rubbing his face. 'Matte required more from us. We did the best that we could.'

'Are you sure?' said Britten. Her eyes were shiny with tears. 'Did we really do our best? Couldn't we have tried harder? Tried to help them both? Given Lisette the time and the attention that she deserved? Now I'm afraid it's too late.'

Harald fixed his eyes on his coffee as he shook his head. 'I suppose I could have worked less . . .' he said. Britten realized that this was the first time she'd ever heard him mention that possibility. She thought of all the times she'd told him that he didn't need to work so hard, sometimes pleading with him, sometimes shouting at him in anger. But now that he'd said the words out loud, she realized how unrealistic that would have been. Harald might not be the most brilliant of men – that was a fact she'd accepted long ago. But he loved to work, and to work hard. That was all he knew how to do, and he couldn't live any other way. So maybe he was right. Maybe they'd done the best they could, in the circumstances.

'What do we do now?' she asked, again putting her hand over Harald's.

'We leave them alone for a while. Later, once we're off this island, we'll find some sort of solution. It'll all work out.'

They drank their coffee in silence. There was nothing more to say.

Martin gave a start as another rumble of thunder sounded overhead. He'd always been afraid of thunder. It was embarrassing, now that he was a grown man, but there was something about the flash of lightning that illuminated everything with its horrible glare, and then the waiting . . . the waiting for the boom that he knew would follow. Silently he began counting after the lightning lit up the kitchen. One thousand one, one thousand two, one thousand three . . . 'Pow!' Martin flinched. Bernard had sneaked up behind him and was now smiling at him with that nasty expression of his. 'Sorry. Did I scare you?' He laughed. The real thunder rumbled, sounding more distant.

'Not at all,' said Martin dismissively.

'When's lunch?' asked Bernard, turning to Kerstin and Börje. He made the question sound as though he was speaking to servants.

'In half an hour,' replied Kerstin, before going back to her work preparing the food.

'Good. That means we have time to talk.' Bernard motioned to Martin, who reluctantly followed him out of the kitchen. No matter how unpleasant Martin found the man, he had to admit that Bernard did possess a great deal of authority. It would be hard not to obey Bernard Liljecrona.

'What's this about?' asked Martin in an attempt to regain control.

Bernard cast a glance at Harald and Britten, who were sitting at the far end of the dining room, but he didn't reply. With long strides he headed for the office, and for a moment Martin thought that Bernard was intending to sit down behind the desk and start interrogating him. Fortunately, he sat down in the visitor's chair instead, giving Martin a challenging look.

Against his will, Martin found his curiosity piqued. He took his seat behind the desk and raised his eyebrows, signalling for Bernard to tell him what was on his mind.

'You saw what just happened,' said Bernard, his voice dry and matter-of-fact.

'You mean the . . . fight between you and Matte?' Martin wondered where this conversation was headed. He had his suspicions.

'Yes. You saw how Matte attacked me. And it was more or less unprovoked.'

Martin questioned how 'unprovoked' it had really been, but he remained silent, waiting for Bernard to continue.

'This is nothing new. Matte has had certain . . . problems.' Bernard paused for a moment, then went on. 'Harald and Britten have done their best to keep it under control, to hide it – and Ruben did his part, too. But the truth is, Matte has always been unstable. He's even been locked up a few times . . . And, well . . . If I were looking for the most likely murderer in this group of people . . .' He threw out his hands.

Martin sighed. He'd been hoping that Bernard would give him something more substantial. The fact that Matte had psychological problems was not news, and it did nothing to move the investigation forward.

'Do you have anything more concrete to tell me?' said Martin wearily.

'What do you mean, "more concrete"? He tried to strangle me! What could be more concrete than that? It was attempted murder, goddammit!'

'I'd say that calling it "attempted murder" is going a bit far. And even if it were, there's nothing to link this incident to Ruben's death. Besides, everyone has said that Ruben and Matte were very close. So why would he want to kill him?'

Another crash of thunder. Bernard and Martin both flinched.

Bernard grunted. 'You can talk all you want about motive, but who can understand the workings of a sick mind? The fact that they were so close just makes it more plausible. Don't you agree?'

'What do you mean?' asked Martin, though he couldn't muster much enthusiasm.

'Love can so easily turn to hate. An unstable person like Matte can easily start imagining things, and who knows what he might have been thinking about Grandpa.'

'Hmm . . . Doesn't sound very convincing, in my opinion,' said Martin, shaking his head. 'I've made a note of what you've told me, but I'll need proof before I put Matte's name at the top of the list of suspects.'

'All right, but I'm thinking of filing a formal complaint as soon as we get off this island. He can't attack me like that and get off scot-free.' Bernard leaned forward to glare at Martin.

'You're fully within your rights to do that,' he replied, standing up to indicate that the conversation was over.

Bernard's response was drowned out by another loud clap of thunder, and this time it sounded much closer.

Lunch was eaten in silence. While Lisette had sullenly re-emerged from her room, Matte remained conspicuously absent. The food that Kerstin and Börje served was both tasty and well-prepared, yet no one seemed in the mood to enjoy it.

Martin wondered what Harald and Britten would say if they knew that Bernard had tried to pin the murder on their son. Not that he was about to tell them. He stole a glance at Lisette, who was seated next to him, her eyes obstinately fixed on her plate. She hadn't exchanged a single word with him since she'd come downstairs, and he realized once more that they had passed the point where their relationship could be repaired. And that was fine with him. In the meantime, so long as they were stuck on the island, things were bound to be frosty between them.

He leaned towards Harald and Britten who sat across from him and said quietly, 'Have you spoken to Matte?'

They both shook their heads.

'No,' said Britten after a glance at her husband. 'We wanted to give him some time alone. He usually calms down after a while if he's left in peace.'

'Maybe we should go upstairs and look in on him,' said Harald in a subdued voice.

'No. Leave him be,' said Britten, although she didn't seem convinced. Harald didn't insist, and everyone continued eating their lunch in strained silence. The only sound was the clinking of forks and knives on the china plates.

Martin felt panic growing inside him. He wanted desperately to get out of this building and away from this island. Above all, he wanted help with the investigation, the assistance of someone more experienced who could advise him on how to proceed and point out leads that he had missed. Right now he had absolutely no idea who had murdered the old man. He was no closer to solving the case than he'd been the day before, and he was beginning to seriously doubt his own competence.

'I think I'll take a little afternoon nap after lunch,' said Harald, patting his paunch.

'That sounds like a good idea,' replied Martin,

stifling a yawn. There was something about the oppressive mood in the hotel, combined with all the food and drink he'd consumed, that made him feel extremely tired. Even though he'd already taken an hour-long nap.

'I'm going upstairs to lie down,' he told Lisette as he got up from the table. She muttered a reply but still refused to look at him.

A short time later, as Martin was lying on the bed, he heard one door after another open and close. The other guests seemed to have decided to follow his example. The last thing he heard before sleep overcame him was the sound of rolling thunder outdoors.

Britten awoke with a strong feeling that something wasn't right. She tried to shake off her uneasiness, telling herself it must be due to an unpleasant dream, but the feeling remained. She sat up and listened. All she could hear was Harald snoring next to her in the bed and the thunder outside. She'd never known such terrible weather. Every once in a while it looked as if the storm might abate, only for it to get worse. She thought it must have been the thunder that woke her, but she wasn't sure. She sensed it was something else.

She lay down and tried to go back to sleep. But it was no use. She sat up again.

Harald made a snuffling noise and turned onto his side. When he was sound asleep no storm in the world, no matter how loud, was going to wake him. Britten swung her legs off the bed and set her feet on the floor. She was wearing stockings, but she could still feel how cold the floor was under the soles of her feet.

Worry about Matte suddenly struck her with such force that she almost felt ill. Her concern for her son was a constant in her life. It had started the moment he was born and had never ceased. What Lisette didn't understand was that Britten felt just as worried for her as for Matte. And just as much love. But her feelings for her daughter had never been given full expression. Matte had required so much more attention than Lisette. And so much more effort.

Britten sighed. Then she stood up and put on her cardigan. She could hear nothing to indicate that anyone else was awake. It was almost eerily quiet.

Slowly she walked over to the door, not sure what she planned to do. Lisette had stretched out on the sofa in the library, and Britten didn't want to wake her. She didn't have the energy for any sort of discussion with her at the moment. Not when she was feeling so uneasy.

Out in the corridor she made up her mind to look in on Matte. If he was asleep, she would merely stroke his hair, as she'd done so often when he was a boy. If he was awake, she'd have a brief chat with him, just to make sure that he was all right.

Cautiously she pressed down the door handle

to his room. Maybe she should have knocked first, but she was almost hoping to find him asleep. Britten wanted to sit on the edge of his bed and look at his face as he slept peacefully, to see how all the different faces that had come and gone over the years were mirrored in his adult face. Matte as a baby, as an inquisitive five-year-old, as an ever-curious ten-year-old, as a sulky teenager.

She pulled open the door and stepped inside. And screamed.

Vivi couldn't sleep. She'd been lying in bed and staring at the ceiling for almost an hour. Gustav had dozed off in a matter of seconds, as usual. This was how things had always been. He fell asleep at once, while she lay awake for hours, staring into the dark. She hadn't felt like taking a nap after lunch, but everyone else had disappeared, so she hadn't had much choice.

Someone was out in the corridor. Vivi propped herself up on her elbows to listen more closely, and after a few seconds she heard a door open. The scream that followed didn't sound human. It sounded like an animal howling with pain, and the shock made her heart pound in her chest.

'What? What the hell?' Gustav jolted awake and sat up to stare wide-eyed around the room. 'What the hell is going on?' he asked, more alert now.

'I don't know,' Vivi told him, jumping out of bed to pull on her dressing gown, which she'd hung on the bedpost. The scream went on and on, rising and falling, broken intermittently by loud sobs.

Vivi opened the door and stepped out into the hall, followed closely by Gustav, clad only in an undershirt and boxer shorts. Doors were opening and everyone else emerged, looking equally dazed.

'What's happening?' said Harald, heading towards them. At that moment he turned to look at Matte's room and realized where the sound was coming from. He strode over to the door, yanked it open, and then staggered back. On the floor sat his wife with Matte's head resting on her lap. She was rocking to and fro, screaming non-stop. Her lap was spattered with blood, as were her hands, which were holding Matte's head. The blood was from a massive hole in his chest. At first Vivi couldn't take her eyes off that hole and all the blood as she stood in the doorway behind Harald, who began to sway, mute with shock. Then Vivi shifted her gaze to Matte's face. His eyes were open, and she heard rather than felt herself gasp. Matte was staring straight at her, and for a moment she thought he was alive. But then she realized that there was no sign of life in his eyes. Only emptiness and death.

Harald took a few steps into the room and fell to his knees next to his wife. He too began sobbing as he clumsily stroked Matte's arm, as if to convince himself that this was really happening. He tried to put his arm around Britten, but she shook it off and continued to rock and utter shrieks that pierced them all to the core. Vivi shuddered, unable to take in what she was seeing.

Someone tried to push past her. It was Martin Molin.

'What's going on?'

The same question, asked for a third time, and then he too stopped in mid-stride. But he quickly regained his composure and dropped to his knees beside the dead man. There was no need to feel for a pulse. There could be no doubt that Matte was dead.

'He's been shot,' Martin concluded, and it was only then that everyone understood what had caused the hole in Matte's chest. Someone gasped for breath. It was Miranda, who had come to stand next to Vivi.

'Did anyone hear the gunshot?' asked Martin. No one said a word. But several people shook their head in reply.

'How is that possible?' Vivi heard herself say. 'Why wouldn't we have heard the shot?'

'Because of the thunder,' Miranda told her. 'The thunder must have drowned out the sound.'

Martin nodded. 'That sounds plausible. If the shot was fired at the same instant as a loud clap of thunder, it could have masked the noise.'

'Was it a pistol?' Miranda asked.

Vivi could feel the young woman shaking as they stood there, shoulder to shoulder. She moved away a few centimetres so they were no longer touching and pulled her robe tighter around her body. Her secret hammered inside of her. She didn't dare look at Miranda.

Martin got up and began searching the room. He lifted the covers and then bent down to peer under the bed, but found nothing. He straightened up and went over to check inside the fireplace, but there were only charred pieces of wood. Nowhere did he see a gun.

'The murderer must have taken it,' he said at last. 'It's not here in the room, at any rate.' Then he turned to the others. 'I want everybody to keep out of this room.'

Those who were standing in the doorway took a step back. Harald and Britten stayed where they were, sitting on the floor. Britten was now whimpering, and the sound was almost more heart-rending than her screams had been.

Martin squatted down next to Britten and spoke to her in a calm, clear voice, as if talking to a child.

'I need to see what happened. Could you leave me here with Matte for a little while? Just a short time?'

He laid his hand on Britten's shoulder. She didn't shake it off. Martin waited as she continued to rock with Matte's head on her lap. Then she abruptly stopped, gently placed her son's head on the floor, and stood up. She staggered and almost fell, but Harald grabbed her. After a glance from Martin, he put his arm around his wife and slowly led her out of the room.

'It's all right, sweetheart. We need to let Martin do his job. It's all right.'

The family members standing in the corridor moved aside to let them pass. Harald didn't look at them as he led Britten over to the stairs. For a moment everyone stood as motionless as statues, then they followed them downstairs. The image of Britten's bloody hands had been etched into everyone's mind.

As soon as he was alone, Martin searched the room again, this time in a more meticulous manner. He knew that under normal conditions he would have been lynched by his colleagues if they'd caught him tramping about a crime scene the way he was doing now. But extraordinary circumstances required extraordinary measures. He had no choice but to try on his own to find what he could.

He started by crawling about on the floor, slowly, centimetre by centimetre. The whole time he kept his eyes peeled, looking for anything that seemed out of place, but there was nothing. He lifted the covers to peer under the bed. Again, nothing. Two pairs of shoes had been neatly placed next to the door, and all the clothing had been hung up in the wardrobe, which stood against one wall. Matte appeared to have been a very orderly person.

Martin turned one hundred and eighty degrees and then made the same methodical inspection of that part of the room, keeping his face close to the floor to discover even the smallest item. At first he found nothing of interest, but after shifting his gaze slightly to the left, he caught sight of a shiny object under the bedside table. He crawled over and stuck his hand underneath. His fingers touched something hard and cold. It was a mobile phone. One of the fancier models, he noted. He thought he remembered seeing another mobile in the room, and when he glanced at the top of the bedside table, he discovered that he was right. There he saw a cheaper and more worn phone, and Martin guessed that it belonged to Matte. He didn't yet know who owned the other one.

He put the shiny phone next to Matte's on the bedside table and continued his search. When nothing more turned up on the floor, Martin directed his attention to the victim's body. A shiver ran through him when he touched Matte's skin. The whole weekend was fast becoming a crash course in how to handle a corpse. First he studied the wound in the man's chest. This wasn't exactly his area of expertise, but he noticed that the flesh around the wound was black, so he was fairly certain that the gun had been fired at close range. Cautiously he turned Matte onto his side and saw that the bullet had passed right through his body. Then he lay Matte back down and stood up to survey the room. Judging by the position of the body, the bullet had to be somewhere near the door, which was still standing open. He reached out and closed it. And there it was. The bullet had lodged in the wood, but it hadn't gone in very deep. The force of the bullet must have slowed considerably as it passed through Matte's body. Martin didn't touch it. He would let the crime scene techs deal with it when they arrived.

He returned to the centre of the room and frowned. One thing struck him as odd. He'd noticed it earlier, but hadn't stopped to mull it over. Now Martin squatted down. Tiny pieces of stone along with a few bigger chunks lay on the fireplace hearth. He stood up. Something had made a big gash in centre of the mantelpiece. If he hadn't found the bullet in the door, he would have thought the gunshot had caused the damage to the mantel. But that wasn't possible. Matte had a bullet hole in his chest, and there was no sign that more than one shot had been fired. The damage to the fireplace must have been caused by something else. But there was no indication that the shot had been preceded by any sort of scuffle. The rest of the room was nice and tidy. The only thing out of place was the damaged mantelpiece and the bits of stone on the hearth. How strange. On the other hand, the damage might have occurred before Matte was killed. Martin sighed. What a hopeless situation. If only he'd had a colleague with whom he could have discussed everything. On his own, he felt totally at a loss.

He opened the door again and backed out of the room. There was nothing more he could do for the moment. The priority was to move Matte's body to the cold-storage room, to be kept there temporarily along with Ruben's body. Martin was not looking forward to asking the others for help with the task.

Lisette was having a hard time sleeping. The sofa was comfortable enough, but bad dreams kept disturbing her. She'd put in earplugs so as not to hear the roar of the storm outdoors, but the subsequent silence allowed space for too many thoughts, too many worries.

Nightmarish images tormented her. Faces melting together. Ruben turning into Bernard who then turned into Matte. Accusatory eyes. Mournful eyes. Despairing eyes. Eyes directed towards her with anger and hatred. Behind her closed lids, her own eyes shifted about nervously. Something was trying to penetrate the earplugs, a sound. Screams of pain and desperation. But the borderland between dream and reality was blurred, and the screams became part of her dreams. They seemed well suited to the eyes that were haunting her sleep.

In spite of the awful dreams, she fought to stay asleep. Reality was little better, and there was not much she wanted to see when she awoke. Yet sleep had already begun to desert her when she felt a hand on her shoulder. Dazed, she opened her eyes to see her father's face. But his features were so contorted that she hardly recognized him. She sat up with a jolt.

'What's the matter, Pappa?' She instinctively knew that something was terribly wrong. She thought of the screaming in her dream that had seemed so real. 'Tell me. What is it?' She grabbed Harald's arm. Only now did she notice that the library was full of people. Everyone was there. She saw her mother huddled on a big easy chair, and panic seized hold of her. She clung to her father's arm as he sank onto the sofa beside her. 'What's happened?' She looked at the others, and slowly it dawned on her. Everyone was there . . . Everyone except for . . .

'Matte!' she shouted. 'Where is Matte?' She made a move to get up, but her father held her back by putting his arms around her. The gesture was intended both to comfort and to restrain her.

'Something has happened. Something horrible, Lisette.' His voice broke, and Lisette realized this was the first time she'd ever seen her father cry. That alone was enough to set off alarm bells.

'Where's Matte?' she asked again, but her voice sounded feeble and lifeless. She already knew. It was written on their faces.

'Matte is dead,' said Harald, confirming what her mind was struggling to comprehend.

She began sobbing, though with a strange feeling that she was in the grip of a dream. This couldn't be happening. Not Matte. All the bitterness that she'd felt towards him ebbed out of her and disappeared, as if it had never existed.

'How did he die?' She could feel her hands shaking uncontrollably.

'He was shot,' Harald told her, placing his big, warm hand over hers.

'Who did it?' she asked as she attempted to formulate all the questions that were swirling through her head.

'We don't know.' Harald rubbed his other hand over his eyes. It suddenly occurred to Lisette how her mother must be feeling, and she got up to kneel at Britten's feet. She laid her head on her mother's lap and wept as she patted her hands. Britten had stopped screaming and crying; she seemed to be in a state of shock. She stared straight ahead as she absently stroked Lisette's hair.

'I'm going to need some help,' Martin said, appearing in the doorway. His face was ashen, and he avoided looked at Britten, as if her pain was too much for him to handle at the moment. It took a few seconds before the others realized what he meant. Harald was the first to stand up. Gustav went over and put his hand on his brother's shoulder. He did it clumsily, as though unaccustomed to such a display of emotion, yet the gesture was clearly intended to offer sympathy.

'We'll take care of this, Harald. Stay here with your family.' Gustav nodded to Bernard, who silently returned the nod, and then both of them followed Martin out of the room. Gustav closed the door behind them. The others didn't need to see what they were about to do.

'What's happening?' Britten asked in a pre-occupied voice.

Lisette took her mother's hands in her own.

'You mustn't worry about it, Mamma.'

'Are they moving Matte? Where are they going to put him? I need to find him a blanket so he doesn't get cold.' Britten made a move as if to get up. Gently Lisette pressed her back onto the armchair.

'They'll take good care of him, Mamma. I promise. There's nothing more you can do.'

'But . . .'

'Shh . . .' Lisette squeezed in next to her mother in the big chair. She put her arms around Britten and rocked her like a child. She felt as if someone had reached into her chest and ripped out her heart. But she couldn't allow herself to think about that now. Her mother needed her.

On the other side of the closed door heavy footsteps could be heard on the stairs, making their way down to the ground floor. Lisette and her parents listened to the sound of three pairs of feet move past and then fade away.

When they reached the kitchen, Martin realized that the hotel owners might not know what had happened. The room was empty and there was no sign of either Börje or Kerstin, so they may have missed all the commotion. They'd find out soon enough what was going on. In the meantime, Matte's body had to be put inside the cold-storage room. Martin led the way, managing to free one hand so he could undo the padlock and then pull open the door. He shivered at the abrupt drop in temperature as he backed in. He looked around for somewhere to lay Matte. He didn't think it would be a good idea to leave the body on the floor, but there was only one other option.

'Let's put him on top of the freezer for the time being. Then we can fetch a table from the dining room.'

Bernard and Gustav merely nodded. All three men moved past Ruben, careful to avoid looking at him. They set down Matte's body and then hurried out of the cold-storage room to find a table. None of them wanted to linger inside any longer than necessary.

Several minutes later they placed Matte on a table next to his grandfather. Two men from the Liljecrona family. Both had met a violent death – and someone in this house was the killer, but right now Martin had no clue who it could be. And he found that a shocking thought.

The three men made their way back to the kitchen, reluctant to return to the library to confront the family's grief. Instead they poured themselves some coffee and stood there, silently sipping at the hot brew.

'Do you know whether anyone in the family owns a gun? Do either of you have one?' asked Martin, sounding more brusque than he'd intended. But there was no other way to ask the question.

A few seconds of strained silence ensued as Bernard and Gustav exchanged a glance. Finally

Gustav said, 'My father has always had a gun in his possession. He started keeping one close at hand after the kidnapping attempt fifteen years ago.'

Ah, now he remembered. A little piece of long-forgotten information rolled to the fore of Martin's mind. The Eastern European mafia had tried but failed to kidnap Ruben Liljecrona. The police got wind of their plans and were on the scene when the kidnapping was supposed to take place. The story had made headlines in all the tabloids for weeks.

'He never felt truly safe after that,' Gustav went on. 'So he got himself a gun, and he always kept it nearby.'

'How was he able to obtain a gun licence?' asked Martin, instantly realizing the naivety of the question.

Bernard snorted. 'He never bothered with a damn licence. And it was easy to acquire a pistol.'

'Did many people know that Ruben had a gun and where he kept it?'

'Everyone here knew about it,' said Bernard in the same scornful tone that had irked Martin from the first moment they'd met. 'The whole family knew that Ruben was armed, and that he kept the gun in his briefcase, in a special pocket.'

'And why didn't anyone tell me about this before?' said Martin indignantly. 'A murder occurs here at the hotel – there's a killer among us who has yet to be identified – and it doesn't occur to any of you to tell me that there's a gun in the house?' He was so angry that he was shaking.

'We . . . We probably didn't think . . .' Gustav stammered nervously. 'We've all known about the gun for so long that we didn't . . .' His gaze shifted to the door of the cold-storage room. Martin hoped he was thinking the same thing that he was. If the family had bothered to tell him about the gun, maybe Matte wouldn't be lying in there, dead.

'I'm going upstairs to have a look,' said Martin, slamming his coffee cup down on the worktop. On his way upstairs, he cursed himself for not having searched Ruben's room sooner, but at the time it had seemed more important to interview all the witnesses.

The old man's room was the first one on the right. Martin opened the door and stepped inside. It was the biggest and finest room in the hotel, but that seemed only fitting, since Ruben was the one footing the bill. A canopy bed was the centrepiece of the room. It had not been slept in. Ruben had never had the chance to use it. A large suitcase lay open, revealing two stacks of neatly folded clothing.

Martin squatted down next to the suitcase and began carefully lifting out the contents. Shirts, lamb's-wool sweaters, trousers, and underwear. There were enough items for a fortnight, not just a weekend. But if a person doesn't have to lug the suitcase himself, thought Martin, he can bring as many clothes as he likes. The suitcase held nothing but clothing. Martin ran his hands along the sides and bottom of the now empty suitcase but found no hidden gun. He put all the items back inside as carefully as he'd removed them. He glanced around the room. A briefcase was leaning against the bedside table, and the sight filled him with a glimmer of hope. He sat down on the edge of the bed and placed the briefcase next to him. There was a four-digit code, but it hadn't been closed properly, so he was able to open it. The first things he saw were several plastic folders and a thick stack of documents. He carefully lifted them out and set everything on the bed. The briefcase was completely empty. No gun. He felt around inside and touched a soft piece of fabric. It was the same colour as the lining of the briefcase, so he hadn't noticed it before. He unfolded it and realized that he was most likely looking at a piece of material that had been wrapped around the pistol. So the gun had been inside the briefcase, but now it was gone. Martin stared into space as thoughts flew through his head. Ruben's gun was missing, and it didn't take a genius to realize that it had probably been used to shoot Matte.

After returning the piece of fabric to the briefcase, Martin began going through the documents, hoping to find something that would spark his interest. But there was nothing that seemed to have any connection whatever with the two murders. The minutes of a board meeting, a financial report, a risk analysis regarding a proposed investment. Martin sighed and put all the papers back in the briefcase. Then he sat on the bed for a few moments, letting his mind work. Someone had come into

Ruben's room to fetch the gun. Someone who knew that he had the weapon and where he kept it – which included every single member of the Liljecrona family. He sighed again. He dreaded having to go back downstairs to confront the gloom that had now settled over the hotel. He dreaded having to assume the responsibility that rested so heavily on his shoulders. Then he stood up. He might as well get moving. He couldn't sit here for ever.

Miranda came out into the hall as the front door opened. Cold air and snow gusted into the hall, and she shivered. Kerstin and Börje were all bundled up, and they stomped their feet before stepping inside to shake the snow from their boots.

'Brrr . . . It's freezing out there,' said Börje as he pulled off his gloves. 'But the storm's starting to die down. We went down to the dock to have a look. As soon as it's calm enough for the icebreaker to come out, we'll be able to cross to the mainland.' He moved aside to let Kerstin enter, and they both pulled off the down jackets they'd worn to keep warm in the fierce wind.

Börje was about to hang his jacket on a hook on the wall when he caught sight of Miranda's expression.

'What is it? Is something wrong?'

Kerstin turned, aware that all was not as it should be. At first Miranda could only nod. Sobs welled up in her throat, and she couldn't say a thing. Then she made a great effort, coughing to clear the way for the words that would have to come out.

'There's been . . . Something terrible has . . . Matte . . . He . . .' She heard how the words were spilling out haphazardly, and tried to focus so that she could tell them what they needed to know.

'Matte, he . . . he's dead.' The words echoed coldly off the walls. They sounded so harsh and so final as they issued from her lips, and the lump that had formed in her stomach grew with each syllable. From the library she heard intermittent sobs.

The hotel owners looked as if they'd been struck by lightning.

'What . . . what are you saying?' asked Börje in disbelief. 'What . . .? How . . .?' He too seemed to be having a hard time formulating complete sentences. Kerstin's face had gone white as she stood there behind her husband.

'How could that happen?' Börje shook his head as if trying to erase the words he'd just heard.

Miranda coughed again. She still felt like something was lodged in her throat.

'He was shot.'

'Shot?' Kerstin gasped. Her knees buckled, and she had to lean against the wall.

'Shot?' repeated Börje, with another shake of the head.

'Britten found him in his room,' said Miranda as she turned to look at the closed door of the library.

'Oh, dear God. That poor woman.' Kerstin's voice was filled with sympathy. 'How . . . how is she doing?'

'She's in shock.' A loud sobbing could be heard from behind the closed library door, providing an uncanny counterpoint to what she'd just said.

'That poor woman,' Kerstin said again. She seemed to have regained some of her composure.

'Börje, we need to make sure they have coffee and some sandwiches. They need sustenance. And go check on the fireplace. We don't want them to freeze in there. The least we can do is provide the basic services.' Her brisk tone jolted Börje out of his shocked state, and he quickly took off his boots and ski trousers.

'Of course. I'll see to the fire while you take care of things in the kitchen,' he said and headed for the library. He was about to open the door when he stopped abruptly.

'Where is . . . where is his body?'

'In the cold-storage room,' replied Miranda, her voice quavering. 'He's in the cold-storage room.'

'And nobody knows who . . .?' Börje didn't finish his question.

'No. We don't know who did it,' said Miranda, turning her back on Börje and Kerstin to climb the stairs to her room. She felt an urgent need to be alone for a while.

Britten looked up when the door opened. Börje tactfully paused in the doorway as he awkwardly said, 'I'm so sorry . . .' He didn't know what else to say, but she understood. There were no words that could possibly alleviate her pain.

Then Börje went over to the fireplace and stirred the ashes with a poker before putting on more wood.

'At least it will be a little warmer in here,' he said in a low voice before retreating. 'Kerstin will bring you some coffee and sandwiches,' he added, then he closed the door behind him.

Britten watched him with a listless expression. She couldn't care less about the temperature of the room. She doubted she'd even notice if it dropped below freezing. Her body had shut down, as if it could no longer feel such trivial things as heat, cold, hunger, or thirst. Her brain was processing what she had seen, trying to make sense of the information that was impossible to comprehend. How could she accept that Matte, her boy Matte, was dead?

Lisette was huddled at her feet, her head resting on Britten's lap. She could feel her daughter shaking with sobs as she intermittently stroked her hair. She was incapable of offering comfort to anyone else at the moment. She couldn't even acknowledge their grief. She had enough to do, trying to deal with her own sorrow.

Britten remembered the day he was born. It was in July, and the birthing room was unbearably hot. She caught sight of a wasp that was stuck between the panes of the window, and all the time she was in labour, she kept her attention focused on the insect's struggle. But the second she saw Matte, she forgot about the wasp and her own pain. He was so tiny. He was of normal weight, yet in her eyes he seemed incredibly small and fragile. She counted his fingers and toes several times, as if murmuring an incantation to reassure herself that everything was fine. He didn't cry. She realized in amazement that he'd come silently into this world, with his eyes wide open in surprise, looking a bit cross-eyed as he tried to focus. The instant she saw him, she had loved him so much that she thought her heart would burst. Of course she had loved Lisette too, when she was born a few years later. But Matte was her first-born. And the two of them had shared something special. A unique bond existed from the moment his inquisitive eyes had met hers. Harald was not allowed to be present at the birth – it wasn't the custom back then. And that had merely made the bond between Britten and Matte even stronger. It was the two of them against the world. Nothing was ever going to come between them.

Naturally, things changed as he got older. Those first magical moments could never be recaptured, but remnants of them remained. A feeling that they shared something special. It had pained her to see what a tormented soul he became, and to glimpse the demons that he fought. So many times she had felt nearly suffocated by the constant questions: Was it something she had done? Something they had done? Deep inside she knew that it wasn't their fault. Even during those first, trembling seconds when his tiny body, so warm and sticky, lay on her breast, she had seen a seriousness in his eyes. He was an old soul who had once again come into this world, even though he might have preferred to be left in peace. This was not something Britten could discuss with Harald. But part of her was not surprised when she found him there, lying on the floor, with those lovely blue eyes staring vacantly. Somehow she had always known that the old soul inside of Matte would not last an entire lifetime. It had already seen too much, experienced too much. The fact that Matte had lived for thirty years was more than she'd dared hope for, but that didn't make her grief any easier to bear. She sat there and continued to stroke Lisette's hair.

Martin went into the kitchen just in time to see Kerstin pour the freshly made coffee into a thermos.

'Oh, could I have a cup?' he asked, in search of any sort of stimulant he could find to combat the fatigue and discouragement that he was feeling.

'Of course,' said Kerstin, filling a mug with black coffee. She handed it to Martin and then hesitated a moment before saying, 'We heard about Matte. How did it happen?'

Börje had come into the kitchen and wanted to hear what he had to say too. Martin took a big gulp of the coffee.

'Matte was shot. His mother found him in his room. And as yet we don't know who did it.'

'It must be the same person who murdered Ruben,' said Börje with a frown. He cast a glance at the door to the cold-storage room.

Martin shrugged. 'To be honest, I really have no idea. But I agree that it does seem likely that the same person committed both murders.'

'Have you found the weapon?' asked Börje, studying Martin closely.

'No. There was no gun in Matte's room. And I searched it thoroughly.'

'Is he in there?' asked Kerstin, a tremor in her voice as she nodded towards the cold-storage room.

'Yes, he is. We put him next to Ruben. But we need to get both of them to the mainland soon. And we need to have the crime scene techs out here so they can start doing their job before the evidence disappears.' Martin could hear how frustrated he sounded.

Börje repeated what he'd said to Miranda. 'We've just come back from the dock. It's a hell of a job getting down there because of the snow. Some of the drifts reach up to my waist. But it can be done, and if the weather lets up a little so that the icebreaker can make it through, we can get to the mainland.'

'What about getting the phone line fixed?' Martin didn't hold out much hope, but he still asked the question.

Börje shook his head regretfully. 'We checked the line. It was blown down, and we won't be able to do anything about it until the repair guys come.'

'Okay, then I suppose we'll just have to put all our hopes on the icebreaker,' said Martin. 'How will we know when it gets here?'

'Trust me, we'll hear it,' said Kerstin, who had started making sandwiches. 'It makes an incredible racket when it goes out, and the sound carries up here. So we don't have to worry about missing it.'

'And you're sure that they'll break the ice all the way over here?'

Börje nodded. 'They know that we have guests at the hotel. I talked to them last week. As soon as they can go out, they'll break a path right to the dock.'

'Good,' said Martin, reaching for a ham-and-cheese sandwich. 'Until then, we'll have to manage the best we can. But I hope the storm lets up soon, for everyone's sake.'

All three turned to look at the closed door to the cold-storage room.

After exchanging a knowing look, Gustav and Bernard discreetly left the library, which was where they had gone after helping Martin move Matte's body. Feeling at a loss, both of them had stood in a corner of the room, whispering to each other and uncertain how to behave towards Matte's family. Vivi and Miranda had already gone upstairs to their room, but Bernard and Gustav put on their jackets and went out in the cold. After the claustrophobic atmosphere inside the house, it felt liberating to breathe in fresh air, no matter how cold it was.

'Cigar?' Gustav held out a case of hand-rolled cigars.

'Sure. I suppose they're just as appropriate now as at a festive occasion,' said Bernard, taking a cigar. With a practised hand he cut the end and then lit it, inhaling with pleasure. The cigar tasted heavenly. And it probably wasn't cheap, knowing his father. At home Gustav had a small fortune in cigars stored in a humidor.

Gustav also enjoyed the first puff, closing his eyes as he slowly blew out the smoke.

'So what do you think?' Gustav stared into the darkness, pulling his jacket tighter.

'Hmm . . . What the hell are we supposed to think?' said Bernard, puffing on his cigar. 'The whole thing is like a bad farce.'

'I'm not sure "farce" is the proper word,' said Gustav, giving Bernard a sharp look.

'That's not how I meant it. I just think the whole situation is a bit . . . absurd. Maybe that's a better word.'

'I agree.' Gustav puffed on his cigar. 'Absurd about sums it up. A damned hard blow for Britten and Harald.'

'You're right about that. Tragic.' Bernard tapped some ash from his cigar.

'But what do you reckon? Who killed Ruben and Matte? I have to admit, I wouldn't have thought anyone in this family had the guts to do anything like that.'

Bernard laughed.

'I'm inclined to agree, Pappa. Do you know, for a while I suspected it might be you. But that was before Matte died.'

'Me?' Gustav gave his son an insulted look.

'Yes. I realize how hard Grandpa had been leaning on you lately, and I thought that . . . that maybe you'd decided to take matters into your own hands.' Bernard laughed again as he extinguished his cigar in the snow.

'Now, listen here,' said Gustav indignantly. 'Would I kill my own father? Sometimes I wonder what makes you tick.' He shook his head.

'Consider it a compliment. Everybody else seems to consider you a weakling. The fact that I suspected you means that I at least think there's a man of action hidden in my old dad.'

In spite of himself Gustav was rather pleased by the remark.

'Hmm . . . well, you may be right about that.' He too put out his cigar in the snow. Then he stuck his hands into the pockets of his black duffel coat.

'Do you think Harald might have . . .?' Bernard let the question hover in the air.

Gustav seemed about to protest, but then he paused to give the question serious consideration.

'If it was just Ruben, maybe. But Matte? I can't believe he would shoot his own son in cold blood.'

'But we don't know what happened,' said Bernard. 'Maybe they started to fight, and then the gun went off . . . I'm not saying he did do it, but I wouldn't rule it out.'

'You could be right,' said Gustav reluctantly. 'It's not completely out of the question. Harald also inherited his share of Pappa's . . . hot temper, and he's always been so emotional.' He paused as if to consider what he'd just said.

'Hopefully the police from the mainland will arrive soon. Lisette's boyfriend seems a bit wet behind the ears, so I wouldn't put much faith in him solving the case.' Bernard laughed crudely.

'No, that milquetoast is not up to much.' Gustav also laughed.

'Milquetoast! You sound like you're in one of those old slapstick comedies,' said Bernard as he opened the front door.

'Hey, watch yourself. Don't go insulting your father!' Gustav led the way into the house, and they swiftly dropped all signs of humour as they put on sombre expressions that were more appropriate to the situation.

'Could I have a word with you? Do you mind?' Martin had stuck his head in the library to speak to Harald.

Harald cast an enquiring glance at Britten, who nodded. With one last look at his wife and daughter, he left the room to join Martin.

'I thought we'd sit in the dining room,' said Martin. Harald didn't reply but simply followed. They sat down at one of the tables, and Kerstin discreetly brought each of them a cup of coffee and some sandwiches before she took the rest of the food to the library.

'Have something to eat,' said Martin, moving the platter of sandwiches closer to Harald. He merely grimaced and pushed the plate away.

'I need to ask you a few questions,' said Martin. He felt terrible about having to intrude on the man's grief, but Harald didn't seem to mind.

'Go ahead and ask,' he said wearily, rubbing his hand over his face.

'It has to do with your father's gun,' said Martin, noticing that Harald flinched.

'My father's gun? What does that have to do with—' And then it seemed to dawn on him. 'Is that what . . .?' His face took on an ashen pallor.

'We won't know for certain until the techs have done their job. But the gun is missing, so there's reason to assume that . . .' He didn't finish the sentence. 'Who knew about it?' he went on, wanting Harald to confirm what he'd already been told.

Harald's hand shook as he lifted the coffee cup. 'Everyone in the family. They all knew about it. My father was the subject of an attempted kidnapping fifteen years ago. They were only two days from putting their plan into motion, but then one of the kidnappers got drunk in a pub and said too much to the wrong person. But I know that Pappa was very, very frightened. Maybe for the first time in his life. They had put together a box that they

106

were going to keep him in. Pappa saw a picture of it in the newspapers, and the next day he made arrangements to obtain a gun. He always carried it with him. The whole family knew about it.'

'He seems to have kept it in his briefcase.'

'Yes. That's right.'

'Did he keep the briefcase locked?' Martin reached for a sandwich.

'That was a bone of contention with the rest of the family. He usually neglected to lock it. The briefcase has a combination lock, but he seldom bothered to use it. We'd scold him about it, partly because of the gun and partly because of the confidential documents that he kept inside. There are people who'd do anything to get hold of that sort of information. But he was oddly careless about it.'

'And was this something that was generally known within the family?'

'Yes.' Harald shook his head in disbelief. 'But I can't imagine . . . I mean, who would . . . who in the family would even think about doing something like that? Matte, who never hurt a fly.' His eyes filled with tears.

Martin hated asking the question, but he had to do it.

'It looked as if he did a good job of attacking Bernard earlier today.'

'He was provoked,' snapped Harald, but the anger vanished as quickly as it had flared up, and he added in a subdued voice, 'I've always had the feeling that there was some old quarrel between

Bernard and Matte, and I . . . I should have tried to find out what it was.' He abruptly sat up straight. 'Do you think that Bernard is the one who . . .?' His face suddenly regained some colour.

Martin held up his hands. 'I'm not making any assumptions at the moment. And we don't want to make the situation worse with false accusations.' He gave Harald a stern look.

'I hear what you're saying,' he said with a nod. 'I'll keep my thoughts to myself. But if there's the slightest evidence.' His eyes narrowed.

'Evidence.' The word stirred something in Martin's memory. There was some detail that he'd missed. Something he should have done, or seen, but right now it escaped him. He focused on the word again: evidence. That was it! He needed to get back to Matte's room.

'Excuse me, Harald, but there's something I need to check. Thank you for your help.' He got to his feet and was halfway out the door when he stopped and said kindly, 'Try to eat.' Then he dashed into the hall and up the stairs.

Vivi knocked timidly on Miranda's door. Her daughter's room was across from the one that she shared with Gustav, and she'd heard the door open and close not long ago. She'd been lying on the bed, on top of the covers. Staring at the ceiling and letting her thoughts wander. Chaotic, dark thoughts. Every time she closed her eyes, she saw Matte's dead body. The blood in the middle of his chest and on the floor. Britten's expression as she rocked her son's head on her lap. Finally Vivi refused to close her eyes again. The images were less intense and less frightening if she focused her gaze on the ceiling. Her own guilt sat like a weight on her chest. Her fear had safeguarded the secrets, but now they were fighting to resurface. She wasn't sure why. She'd never felt any longing to clear her conscience; she'd decided long ago to take the secrets with her to the grave. But now everything was different. Maybe because she'd been confronted by death at close range. Maybe it was the look on Britten's face. Nothing could be worse than that. Compared with the pain of losing a child, everything else seemed so petty. Including the secrets. 'Trolls crack in the sun,' as her mother had always said. For the first time it felt as if the sun was shining on her secret, making it seem small and insignificant. She got up. An unaccustomed feeling of decisiveness came over her. She had never made an unpleasant decision in her whole life; she had always tried to keep the path ahead wide open and smooth. Now she was about to throw fuel on a fire that no one even knew about.

She put on her cardigan and stuck her feet in her slippers, which she had placed neatly next to the bed. For a moment she hesitated before opening the door, but once she stepped out into the hall, she knew there was no turning back. It was time.

In a few short steps she reached the door to Miranda's room and tapped lightly on the wood.

At first she heard a rustling, and then her daughter's voice saying, 'Who is it?'

'It's me.'

The sound of footsteps, and then Miranda opened the door with a concerned look of enquiry. 'Has something else happened?'

Vivi shook her head. 'No, nothing.' Then she hesitated before asking, 'Can I come for a minute?'

'Of course. Come on in.' Miranda moved aside to let her mother into the room. 'I was only lying on the bed reading. I needed to get away from . . . from everything.' A shadow flitted across her face, and Vivi wondered if she was doing the right thing. But her doubt vanished as swiftly as it had appeared. It was time to clear the air, empty out the wardrobes, and let the old skeletons see the light of day.

'There's something I have to tell you.' Vivi sat down on her daughter's bed.

'What is it?' said Miranda, sitting down next to her mother.

'I . . .' The words refused to come out, and Vivi raised her hand to her throat, as she usually did when nervous. All of a sudden she wasn't sure whether to continue. Or how she should formulate what she wanted to say. She cleared her throat.

'I did something very stupid. Many years ago. But I've always regretted it,' she hastened to add. Miranda stared at her in surprise. She had absolutely no idea what her mother was talking about.

'I had . . . I had a brief affair. With another man. And I ended up pregnant.'

Miranda's eyes opened wide. She raised her hands, like a child trying to fend off something upsetting, something she did not want to hear. But then she let her hands drop to her lap, staring mutely at Vivi.

'Your father knows nothing about it. He did notice that you arrived a little early, but men . . . well, they're good at fooling themselves. Sometimes I wonder whether he might have guessed, but I don't think so.' She sniffed.

'So you're saying that I'm . . .' Miranda swallowed hard, her eyes still fixed on her mother. Vivi could almost see her brain working to take in this information.

'Yes, I'm saying that Gustav isn't your biological father.' Vivi was amazed how easy it was to say those words that had been concealed in her heart for so many years. She had guarded them with such vigilance, preventing them from seeping out, preventing herself from even thinking what they signified. And here she was, telling her story in a calm and matter-of-fact voice. She felt a great sense of relief spreading through her body. Only now did she realize how heavy a burden it had been.

'Then who?' Miranda paused. Her hands were moving restlessly like little birds on her lap.

'Harald.' Vivi plucked at a nub on the coverlet. 'Harald is your father. We had a very brief affair. I broke it off when I realized that I was pregnant.'

Miranda gasped loudly.

Vivi went on: 'I'm the only person who knows

111

about this, although it's possible that Harald guessed the truth. But I want you to know that Matte was your brother, not your cousin.' She felt almost dizzy with relief as she heard the words come bubbling out. It was as if everything that had happened this weekend – the tragedy of Ruben's death and Matte's death – had set her free. What was there left to fear now that the heavens had already come tumbling down?

'Matte . . . was . . . my . . . brother?' Miranda stammered. 'I can't believe—' She shook her head but didn't take her eyes off her mother. 'But how . . . when?'

'We can talk more about this later,' said Vivi, patting her daughter's hand. 'But first you need to think about all this in peace and quiet. Then you can ask me questions. At least now you know.'

As Vivi stood up to leave, she and Miranda both heard someone running up the stairs. Vivi opened the door to the corridor and almost collided with Martin as he raced past.

'Sorry,' she said, but he didn't seem to notice. She saw him stop when he reached Matte's room, and she wondered why he was in such a hurry.

Martin was cursing himself. How could he have been so damned sloppy? He had found evidence, possibly the only piece of evidence, and he'd left it in the room. What if the murderer had already come back to get it?

He swore as he yanked open the door to Matte's

room. Then he paused to calm down as he caught sight of the pool of blood on the floor. It would only make matters worse if he rushed into the room and began stomping around, disturbing any prints. Instead he moved cautiously towards the bedside table. He didn't realize he was holding his breath until he exhaled with relief when he saw what was lying on the table. The mobile phone. The second phone. Not Matte's, but someone else's.

He opened the cover. The phone was switched off, and he would need the password to turn it on and find out whose it was. Shit! He flipped the phone closed but took it with him as he left the room. Slowly he made his way down the stairs and then paused for a few seconds outside the door to the library. Then he pushed it open and went in. As soon as he entered the room he sensed the grief, almost like a physical barrier. For a moment he considered turning and leaving so as not to disturb anyone. Yet he knew that he had no choice.

He cleared his throat to draw attention.

'Is there really no way for us to leave this place?' Britten's voice sounded so feeble and frail. It barely reached Martin, standing two metres away, before fading completely.

He shook his head. 'Not yet. But Börje and Kerstin went down to the dock, and as soon as the storm lets up a bit, the icebreaker will be out.'

'Can we take Matte with us when we go?' Britten drew the blanket tighter around her shoulders. Martin saw that she was so cold that her teeth were chattering, even though the fire in the grate had warmed up the room.

'We'll see to it that he comes with us,' said Martin, hoping that it wasn't a mistake to make that promise. But he'd just have to bear the consequences of that decision later on. He didn't have the heart to refuse her request when she looked as if she might fall apart at any moment.

'I have a question for all of you. Does anyone recognize this?' He held up the mobile phone.

'That's mine,' said Bernard at once. 'Where did you find it?'

'In Matte's room.'

Bernard's face was expressionless. 'How did it end up there?'

'Exactly what I want to ask you,' said Martin, fixing his eyes on Bernard.

'I have no idea. The last time I saw it, it was in my room. I didn't feel the need to carry it around, since there's no reception.'

'And when was that?'

'This morning, when I woke up,' replied Bernard. 'I was using it as an alarm clock.'

'Have you been in Matte's room today?' Martin was aware he sounded brusque, but he was so stressed that he wasn't able to hold his emotions in check any more.

'No, I've never been inside Matte's room! Are you accusing me of something?' Bernard took a step forward, but his father placed a hand on his arm to restrain him.

'Martin is only doing his job, Bernard. Take it easy. We all want to get to the bottom of this.' Gustav glanced at Britten, who was staring straight ahead as if she hadn't registered what was being said.

Bernard shook off his father's hand but repeated in a lower voice, 'I haven't been inside Matte's room. Not once.'

'So you have no idea how your mobile got there?'

'Someone must have been in my room and taken it,' said Bernard with a frown. 'That's what must have happened. Someone wanted to shift suspicion onto me. The killer must have gone in and taken my phone and then put it in Matte's room.'

'Shall we go upstairs and have a look at your room?'

'Of course.' Bernard threw out his hands and then headed for the door. 'I have nothing to hide. Look around as much as you like.' His tone was scornful, and Martin had to resist an urge to kick the man as he walked past.

He followed Bernard up the stairs. At the top they met Vivi and Miranda, who were on their way down. Both women wore a strange expression, but Martin had no time to wonder why.

'What are the two of you doing?' Vivi asked Bernard.

'Nothing. We're just going to check on something,' said Bernard evasively as he continued on to his room. Martin was right on his heels.

'See, it's not locked. Anybody could go in.' Bernard opened the door and motioned for Martin to enter.

The room was immaculate. Three white shirts, meticulously pressed, hung in the open wardrobe. A pair of shiny black shoes, identical to the ones Bernard was wearing, had been placed underneath the shirts. No suitcase was visible, so it must have been stowed away. A book lay on the bedside table. *The Adventures of Sherlock Holmes*. Martin was just thinking to himself that he wouldn't have taken Bernard for a reader, when Bernard stopped short and said:

'That's Grandfather's book, I can't imagine what it's doing here. I only read business publications. Grandpa was the one who was so keen on Sherlock Holmes. Those stories seem incredibly lame, in my opinion.'

Martin raised an eyebrow. 'Do you notice anything else odd? Is anything else missing?'

Bernard looked around but then shook his head. 'No, everything else is exactly as I left it.'

Martin knelt down to lift up the bed covers.

'What are you doing?' asked Bernard in surprise. 'Oh, you're looking for the gun.'

'Yes,' said Martin, squinting to peer under the bed and all the way over to the wall. 'Any objections?'

'No, damn it. Knock yourself out!' Bernard leaned against the wall, crossed his arms, and watched with amusement as Martin crept about on the floor.

After a few minutes Martin stood up, brushed off his trousers, and said, 'I assume you brought a suitcase. Can I see it?'

'Be my guest,' said Bernard, and pointed at the wardrobe. 'It's in there. Go ahead and paw through my underwear.'

Martin pulled the suitcase out of the cramped space, placed it on the floor, and opened the lid. He rummaged through the clothes and searched the side pockets but found nothing.

'No smoking gun?' said Bernard, watching as Martin put the suitcase back in the wardrobe.

'No,' said Martin. 'I didn't find a thing.'

'Am I still your primary suspect?' Bernard seemed to be genuinely enjoying the situation.

'You're at the top of the list, at any rate. So don't leave town, as they say.'

'No risk of that.' Bernard laughed. 'Although it sounds as though the bloody storm is starting to abate at last. Maybe it won't be long before we can leave this godforsaken place.'

'Let's hope so.' Martin looked around one last time before he left the room. Bernard followed.

'Can I have my phone back?' asked Bernard, holding out his hand.

'No. I'll keep it for the time being,' Martin told him, patting his pocket. 'There's still no phone reception, so you won't be needing it.'

'What about the book?'

'I'm going to ask the others whether anyone knows anything about it. But I'd be surprised if anyone voluntarily admits to putting it in your room. What do you think? Is it some sort of message to you?'

'Or maybe I put it there myself. To throw you off the trail. Don't forget that I'm your prime suspect!' He laughed again.

This time Martin couldn't keep silent. 'Do you think the situation is funny? Your cousin is dead. And your grandfather, too. But you seem to regard the whole thing as a joke.'

'I'm crying inside,' said Bernard, melodramatically clutching his hand to his chest.

Martin couldn't stand looking at him any longer. He pushed his way past and went back downstairs. There he met Börje.

'The storm is letting up,' he said, and Martin nodded. 'Yes, we noticed. Maybe we'll be able to leave soon.'

'Well, we don't really want our guests to be eager to leave. But in this situation I can understand how you all feel.' Börje then pointed towards the library. 'There's fresh coffee.'

'Thanks,' said Martin, and headed in that direction. He heard Bernard coming down the stairs behind him. Martin hurried to enter the library so he wouldn't have to listen to any more idiotic comments.

'What have you been doing?' asked Harald, who had regained some of his authority. He gave Martin a stern look.

'We were checking on something,' he replied

with a dismissive gesture. He planned on telling all of them what they'd found, but he wanted to do it on his own terms.

He went over to the table where the coffee maker had been placed and poured himself a cup. Then he sat down on the sofa. Lisette had moved from where she'd been sitting at her mother's feet and was now slumped on the sofa, staring at the floor with glassy eyes. Martin reached out to stroke her hand, which was resting on the sofa cushion. She didn't respond, but at least she didn't push his hand away. Martin realized that he'd been terribly negligent when it came to his duties as her boyfriend. Or rather, ex-boyfriend. He hadn't even made an attempt to comfort her.

Martin could hear that Bernard was building up to tell his father about the book on the bedside table, so he jumped into the conversation.

'It appears that someone went into Bernard's room earlier today. At least, that's what Bernard claims.' He couldn't resist adding the latter remark. 'And this person seems to have taken a mobile phone and then placed a book on the bedside table. Do any of you know anything about this?' Martin looked around at everyone gathered in the library. Silence was the only reply. Britten didn't seem to have heard the question. Bernard and Gustav merely shook their heads. Vivi and Miranda, who were sitting on the sofa across from him, also seemed preoccupied with other thoughts. Miranda's face was white as a sheet. Martin suddenly remembered that both she and her mother had had an odd look on their faces when he met them on the stairs. That might be something worth checking out.

'What sort of book?' Lisette now asked, turning to look at Martin.

'Sherlock Holmes. An anthology, I think.'

Lisette giggled. A strangely hollow sound. 'It probably belongs to Grandpa. He was obsessed with Sherlock Holmes.'

'In his younger days he was the chairman of a Sherlock Holmes club,' Harald added. 'And he continued to be a member all these years. I've always had a feeling that the club – and the purported interest in those detective stories – was merely an excuse for a bunch of old men to sit around chatting and drinking whisky once a month.'

'No, Ruben was genuinely interested.' Britten's voice still sounded very fragile. 'And he got Matte interested too. They used to discuss the stories whenever they got together on Fridays.'

'But you have no idea who might have put the book there? Or why?'

No one answered.

Gustav cleared his throat. 'No sign of the gun?'

'No. I'm afraid not.'

Silence again settled over the room. Everyone was gathered in the library, and only now did it fully occur to Martin that one of these individuals was a murderer. There was no getting around that. Two men lay dead inside the cold-storage room.

One poisoned, the other fatally shot. Whoever committed the murders was here in this room. Martin felt cold shivers ripple through his body. It was an alarming thought.

'What will happen once we get back to the mainland?' Miranda asked the question that was on everyone's mind.

'All of you will be interviewed by my colleagues at the police station. The tech team will come over here to examine the crime scene.' He hesitated for a moment but then went on.

'The bodies of Ruben and Matte will be taken to the pathology lab for a post mortem. I'm hoping that we'll be able to solve the case relatively quickly.'

Miranda nodded. She looked from one person to the next, and she seemed to be thinking the same thing as Martin. It was as if she was seeing the other family members for the first time, considering them as suspects. Then her eyes alighted on her mother, and that odd expression returned to her face. For her part, Vivi was looking at Martin, and he noticed a sense of calm in her gaze that he hadn't seen before. The nervous and fitful energy that had been so prevalent seemed to have vanished. That made Martin even more curious. He decided to get to the bottom of this.

'Vivi . . . Could I have a word with you? In the office?'

She nodded and stood up to follow him out of the library.

When they were both seated in the small office for the second time that dramatic weekend, he saw a different woman from the one he'd seen at the first interview.

'I have a feeling that something has happened. Something you haven't told me about.' He paused for a second before going on.

'I can't point to anything concrete, but it feels as if . . .' Martin was searching for the right words when Vivi interrupted.

'You're more sensitive than I thought.' Her composure gave her an entirely different personality, and Martin found that he liked this new Vivi. Whatever had caused the change, it was definitely for the better.

'If I tell you that it's a family matter that has nothing whatsoever to do with the murders, will you drop the subject?' She tilted her head and gazed at him intently as she waited to hear his reply.

'No,' Martin told her. 'Right now I'm the one who decides what's relevant and what isn't. So I'd appreciate it if you would tell me everything, even though you'd prefer to keep the matter private.'

'I thought that's what you would say,' replied Vivi. 'Oh well, since Pandora's box has already been opened, I suppose there's no harm in informing the authorities too.' She laughed, and Martin found himself liking this woman more and more. She seemed to have truly come alive. As if a strong and vibrant Vivi had shaken off her fragile shell.

'As you've noticed, something has changed between Miranda and me. That's because a short time ago I told her that she is not Gustav's daughter. Harald is her father.'

Martin's mouth fell open. Whatever he may have been expecting, this was not it. He didn't say a word as Vivi continued:

'I had a brief affair with Harald and ended up pregnant. And the result was Miranda.'

'What about Bernard?' Martin was still having trouble collecting his thoughts.

Vivi snorted. 'Bernard is definitely Gustav's son. He's the spitting image of his father. But I've always thought that Miranda looked a little like Matte.' For the first time since she'd started talking, her voice quavered.

'That's why I . . . Well, I considered it was only right that Miranda should be told that it was her brother who was dead. Not her cousin.'

'And Gustav? Does he know about this?' Martin still could hardly believe what she'd told him. It was like something out of a soap opera.

'Gustav? No, he'd never imagine that I would have the courage to go behind his back. He has always underestimated me. In every regard. I think he'd be mostly . . . surprised. And furious with Harald, naturally.'

'Does Harald know about Miranda?'

Vivi laughed. 'Of course. Harald was present when she was conceived, after all. Although I don't think he has ever been a hundred per cent certain that Miranda is his daughter. But he knows that it's possible.'

'You must have been scared that the whole story would come out.'

Vivi's face softened at Martin's sympathetic tone.

'Yes. I've had my share of sleepless nights. But more than anything . . .' She hesitated, but Martin didn't say a word. 'More than anything, I've been so worried about what would be inherited.'

'Inherited? The money?' asked Martin, looking puzzled. 'Do you mean that Ruben would be upset if he—'

Vivi shook her head. 'No, not the money to be inherited. I meant genetically speaking. Considering all that Matte has been through over the years . . . the constant episodes of depression and everything else. So of course I've worried that Miranda would suffer the same psychological problems.'

'But she hasn't?'

'No, and thank God for that. It seems to be something that affected only poor Matte.'

'How serious were these periods of depression? No one wants to talk about it.'

'No, I'm sure they don't.' Vivi's tone turned bitter. 'That poor boy never had an easy time of it. Britten did her best, but the men in this family tried to ignore what was going on. Even Ruben, who was so fond of Matte, didn't want to acknowledge how serious the boy's mental problems were. He should have had professional help much earlier, and more extensive treatment than he ever received. Not even when he—' The sound of a distant crash stopped her mid-sentence.

They both looked out of the window.

'The icebreaker seems to have started work,' said Martin, but then he encouraged Vivi to pick up where she'd left off. 'You were saying: "not even when he . . ."'

'Right,' said Vivi, turning to look at Martin again. 'Not even when he tried to kill himself. He tried several times, but they refused to acknowledge how dire the situation was. He would be admitted to an institution for "rest and recuperation", but there was never any question of intensive treatment. I think Harald even said once that he "hoped the boy would grow out of the problem".' Now she sounded angry.

A knock on the door interrupted them. It was Börje.

'The icebreaker is on its way. Everyone should pack their bags and head down to the dock ASAP.'

Martin looked at Vivi. 'All right. I think we're done here.'

She nodded and stood up. 'I'll go upstairs and pack. I have to admit, it's going to be a relief to leave this place behind.'

'I couldn't agree more.' Martin followed her out and then went to the room he was sharing with Lisette. She was already there, packing her clothes in a suitcase. Her eyes were red-rimmed.

'How's it going?' he said, putting his arms around her. For a moment she relaxed and pressed closer.

125

Then she pulled away and said, 'I assume this is goodbye. Am I right?' She looked him calmly in the eye.

Martin could only reply, 'Yes, I think so. I suppose it is.'

She stepped forward, took his face in her hands, and kissed him on the cheek.

'I'm sorry for being so stupid,' she said.

'No, not at all. The whole situation has just been so . . . stressful. It's affected everybody, in one way or another.'

'You're a nice man, Martin.' She kissed him again on the cheek. Then she picked up her suitcase and left the room without looking back. For several minutes Martin didn't move. He was filled with an overwhelming sense of relief, but he also felt a twinge of sorrow. Once again he'd seen a relationship crumble, and it was an experience that was starting to wear him down. Was there really no one out there for him?

With a sigh he tossed his belongings into his bag and slung the strap over his shoulder. He'd put Bernard's mobile and the Sherlock Holmes book in two paper bags, which he'd carefully wrapped up in his sweater and placed on top of everything else. The glass from yesterday's dinner was also securely stowed in his sports bag. He had no intention of leaving it behind.

Before he followed the others downstairs, he went to Matte's room and paused in the doorway. He stared at the room, as if willing it to tell him what had happened there. When he turned his head slightly to the left, he saw the bullet embedded in the door. The damage to the front of the fireplace was still bothering him. He had the feeling that it was important somehow. But for the life of him he couldn't work out what it might mean.

Ten minutes later they were all trudging through the snow towards the dock, but it was difficult because of the luggage they were carrying. Börje had gone on ahead, and judging by the sound, he'd had no trouble starting up the boat's motor. They would soon be back on the mainland. After a hasty consultation, they'd agreed to take all the luggage down to the dock first. Then the men would return to fetch the bodies from the cold-storage room. No one was looking forward to that task. From a purely professional standpoint, Martin knew that he ought to tell the family that the bodies should remain where they were. But he was haunted by the look in Britten's eyes when she asked whether Matte would go with them. So he offered no objections to the plan.

On his way back to the hotel, all sorts of thoughts kept swirling through his mind. The gun, the book, the conversations he'd had with the Liljecrona family, the dinner on that first evening when hidden meanings and taunts had flown like sharp arrows across the table. It all merged into one inside his head. Matte and Ruben. Grandfather and grandson, who had a closer relationship than the rest of the family. Meeting every Friday to talk and share thoughts. Two men, one old, the other young. One physically ill, the other suffering mentally. Their interest in Sherlock Holmes. Martin had only seen films made from some of the stories, and he couldn't understand how anyone could become so obsessed with . . . Suddenly he noticed something hovering at the edge of his consciousness. He came to an abrupt halt in the deep snow, causing Bernard to run right into him.

'What the hell?'

'Oh. Sorry,' said Martin distractedly as he started plodding forward again. They had almost reached the front steps. He shook his head, as if to force the thought to emerge fully, but in vain. It was something connected to the idea of Sherlock Holmes and the films . . . Wait! There it was! He felt a sense of triumph as the thought finally coalesced, and he raced for the door.

'What the hell is the matter with you?' shouted Bernard, but Martin paid no attention. He didn't bother to take off his snow-covered shoes, and he slipped and almost landed on his backside as he stomped indoors. At the last second he managed to grab the handrail and regain his balance. He took the stairs two at a time and ran down the hall towards Matte's room. He could hear the others yelling after him, but he was so focused on what he was doing that their voices barely registered. He had to be right. He knew he was right. It explained everything!

When he opened the door to Matte's room, he

stopped. His heart was pounding so fast in his chest, both from his dash up the stairs and from the excitement at what he now knew. Cautiously he entered the room, walking around the pool of blood on the floor and going over to the fireplace He stared at the missing piece and then reached out to touch it. It was freezing cold. He withdrew his hand and impatiently rubbed his palms together to rub some warmth into them. Feeling a little better, he again reached out one hand and stuck it up the chimney to grope around. At first he found nothing and he was filled with doubt. What if he was wrong? But he kept on searching, and when his fingers touched something hard and cold, he was flooded with relief. So he was right, after all. Now he heard voices behind him.

'What are you doing?' Bernard was standing in the doorway with a perplexed look on his face, his hair uncharacteristically in disarray. Behind him were Harald and Gustav, equally flummoxed.

Without a word, Martin grabbed the object and yanked on it. The men in the doorway gasped when they saw what he was holding.

'The gun?' exclaimed Harald in disbelief. 'But how did it end up in there?'

Still without saying a word, Martin tugged harder to show them that the gun was attached to an elastic band.

'I . . . I don't understand.' Gustav shook his head as he stared at the gun and the elastic band. Martin wasn't ready to start explaining his theory, so he turned his back to them as he continued to search the chimney. Again he looked pleased as his fingers touched plastic. He poked at it carefully, making the plastic rustle faintly, but it refused to give. Then he tried lifting it up, and what turned out to be a plastic carrier bag finally came loose. A perfectly ordinary bag from the ICA grocery store. The bag was heavy, and he carefully set it down on the floor before looking inside. It contained two things: a video camera and an envelope.

By now the three Liljecrona men had come into the room and were standing around Martin. All three looked puzzled.

'Why was a video camera hidden inside the fireplace?' Gustav asked Martin.

'Let's have a look,' he replied, pressing a button on the camera. When it turned on, he pressed Rewind and then Play. At first the display was black, but after a few seconds they heard the familiar voices of Matte and Ruben. Grandpa Ruben was sitting in his wheelchair, speaking directly to the camera. Matte was apparently the one filming the video. Ruben cleared his voice.

'When you see this, I will be dead.'

Harald gasped. Gustav's face had turned white, but Bernard almost seemed amused. As if he already knew what was coming.

Ruben went on.

'I have six months to live, according to my doctors. I'm not in the habit of giving up, so I've consulted every possible specialist, but they all say the same thing. There's no hope. And it's going to be painful. And undignified. As you all know, pain is something I could endure. But an undignified end . . . Never. So I've decided to take matters into my own hands. And I can't resist the chance to tell all of you off. You have betrayed me in the worst possible ways, and you have never lived up to my expectations. Don't worry – you'll get the money. However, knowing you as I do, I doubt the money will make you happy. More likely, it will ruin you. So be it. But I'm not planning to give away the money without making you suffer a little.'

Ruben smiled and reached for something outside the frame of the video. Martin recognized the canopy bed in the background. The film had been made in Ruben's room, here on Valö. Ruben was now holding up a small plastic bag of powder in one hand, level with his face.

'This is potassium cyanide. Not too difficult to obtain, if you have money and the right contacts. I'm going to pour this into my glass tonight at dinner, and hopefully create a dramatic scene. Let me emphasize that I'm going to put it in the glass myself. Matte will not play any role in my death, other than as a supporter and observer. I also want to make it perfectly clear that he has done his utmost to persuade me not to do this. Eventually, realizing how determined I am, he accepted the fact that this is my final wish. He has agreed to help me teach the rest of you a lesson. My hope is that, at least for a short while, you will all suspect and fear that I have disinherited the lot of you. When my will is read, and you discover that your fears are unfounded, Matte is going to make sure that this video is shown. The detective mystery in which you were all involuntary – and innocent – players will at last be solved. "Elementary", as dear Doctor Watson would have said.' Ruben laughed at his own joke, clearly pleased with the plan that he'd cooked up for his own dramatic passage to the other side. Matte was silent as he held the camera, but an occasional shuddering breath revealed how upset he was.

Ruben began shifting about in his wheelchair, apparently getting ready for the finale.

'I wish all of you a hell of a Christmas and a truly miserable New Year. May you have no joy from my money.' He chuckled. Then the screen went black.

'That . . . bastard,' snarled Gustav. Harald was staring vacantly at the display on the video camera, as if he still hadn't fully taken it all in. Bernard started laughing. He laughed harder and harder, until he had to hold his stomach as tears ran down his face. He howled with laughter until his father jabbed an elbow in his side.

'Stop that, Bernard. You're making a fool of yourself.'

'What a bastard,' said Bernard, seemingly unable to stop laughing. 'He fooled us all.' Tears of merriment kept rolling down his face, and he wiped them off on the sleeve of his sweater.

Harald sank down onto the bed. He wasn't smiling.

'But Matte . . . Why?'

Martin handed him the white envelope. 'Maybe this will explain things.'

Harald took the envelope, tore it open with trembling hands, and pulled out a letter. He read it in silence while the others watched.

After a moment he put the letter on his lap and said in a low voice, 'He couldn't live with the fact that he'd helped Grandpa take his own life. Ruben convinced him to do it, begged him to help set up this farce. But he couldn't handle it afterwards. He writes that he couldn't bear knowing what he'd done. And he asks you to forgive him, Bernard. He writes that he took your mobile and put it here in his room so that suspicion would fall on you. But he also knew that as soon as it was discovered that his death was a suicide, you'd no longer be a suspect. He writes that, in that sense, he was truly Ruben's grandson. He couldn't resist a chance for revenge. He wanted to make you suffer.'

'Suicide?' said Gustav. He didn't understand. So Martin explained.

'I suddenly remembered seeing this done in a Sherlock Holmes film. Matte fastened the gun to one end of an elastic band. The other end he attached to the inside of the chimney. Then he shot himself in the heart. As soon as he let go of the gun, the elastic band yanked it up inside the fireplace and out of sight. Abracadabra – the pistol was gone! And our first assumption was that he'd been murdered. It was the gun that made that mark on the mantelpiece,' said Martin, pointing at the gash. 'It rammed into it before it disappeared up inside.'

'I had no idea he was so clever,' said Bernard. He'd stopped laughing, but he still looked amused. 'Well, now that you've worked this whole thing out, I suggest we make our way back to the mainland. The boat is waiting.'

Even though Martin disliked his carefree tone, he knew that Bernard was right. There was nothing more to do here.

Half an hour later the boat pulled away from the dock. Darkness had fallen, but the stars were out, and the boat lights illuminated the snow that was piled high on the ice on either side of the path that the icebreaker had cleared. Everyone now knew what had happened during that weekend on Valö. There was nothing more to say. Everyone sat in silence. Martin turned around so he was sitting with his back to the island that was slowly receding. Up ahead lay Fjällbacka, glittering in the darkness.

On the deck of the boat lay the two dead men, covered with a tarp. It was five days until Christmas Eve.

AN ELEGANT DEATH

'This is bad. Looks like a robbery gone wrong,' said Patrik Hedström as he surveyed the small break room. There was blood everywhere, and a woman's body lay between the kitchen table and the refrigerator. Her eyes stared up at them unseeing, and her skull had been bashed in. Blood had sprayed over the white walls and formed a big pool under the victim's head and torso.

'Yeah. It's bad, all right,' agreed Martin Molin from his position standing behind Patrik.

'Hell of a lot of blood.'

Patrik shook his head. It didn't matter how many times he saw a dead body. It was always the blood that made his stomach heave.

'Somebody must have seen the guy who did this.' Martin's face had lost all colour.

'How do we know it's a guy?' said Patrik. 'It's too early to make that kind of assumption.'

'Sure, I know that, but I was just thinking . . .

with all this violence . . . well, it doesn't seem like something a woman would—'

He stopped himself there. Patrik was right.

'Do you know who she is?' Martin asked instead.

'Lisbeth Wåhlberg. Originally from Fjällbacka, but she's been living in Göteborg for years. Her husband died of a heart attack not too long ago, and then she moved back here. She lives upstairs. Opened this shop only a few weeks ago.'

'So there probably wasn't a lot of cash in the till. At least, not enough to make someone beat her to death to get it.'

'No,' said Patrik. 'You're right about that.'

He ran his eyes over the cramped space. The room next to the shop was sparsely furnished. A cramped kitchen nook with a sink, a coffee maker, and a dish rack that held some cups set out to dry. Near the window stood a small white table with two chairs, and against the wall across from the worktop was a refrigerator. That was it. Except for all the blood. So much blood. And there was something about the blood that gave Patrik pause. Whoever killed Lisbeth must have been in a fit of uncontrollable rage.

Beads of perspiration ran down Erica Falck's face as she struggled to squeeze into the pair of jeans. But no matter how hard she tried, she couldn't get them on.

'Useless crap jeans!' she yelled as she pulled

them off and threw them across the room. Before she'd had children, she'd virtually lived in those jeans. Now she could barely get them past her knees.

She sank down on to the bed wearing only her knickers. A pair of practical white cotton knickers from Sloggi, as she noted in despair. She had to put an end to this slow decline. At the rate things were going, she'd turn into an old lady before she hit forty, with a sensible haircut and fingernails clipped short. She already had the felt slippers, so she could tick off that item. In fact, she had three pairs.

Ten minutes later, having decided that a brisk walk while her mother-in-law Kristina watched the kids would mark the beginning of her new life, she was on her way towards town. As she rounded the corner near the old telegraph office, she came to an abrupt halt. Up ahead there seemed to be something going on, with more police vehicles and more officers than the local department could ever muster. They were gathered outside the small vintage clothing shop that had opened only a few weeks ago. Erica and her sister Anna had both attended the grand opening hosted by the owner.

'Patrik?'

She saw her husband come out of the shop with a grim look on his face. Erica's curiosity got the better of her, and she hurried over to talk to him.

'What are you doing here?' asked Patrik with a frown.

'I was out taking a walk. What happened?' Erica craned her neck in an attempt to peek inside the shop. 'Was it a burglary?' She paid no attention to the fact that Patrik clearly wanted her to leave. By now he ought to have known better than to try to chase her away.

'Erica, I can't—' He was cut off mid-sentence by the appearance of a car that suddenly pulled up at the kerb. Two women jumped out.

'What happened? Where is she?' screamed one of them, an immaculately dressed woman in her forties. The woman behind her looked a bit younger. Concern and alarm were written all over her face.

Erica remembered the two women from the opening. They were Lisbeth Wåhlberg's daughters.

'We can't give out information at this stage,' Patrik began, blocking their way as he took up position in front of the shop door.

'Is Mamma . . .? Is she inside?'

The older sister pointed towards the shop. Patrik took a deep breath.

'I'm sorry to tell you that your mother is dead.'

The older sister let out a shriek. The anguish on the younger sister's face made Erica's heart ache for her.

'We want to talk to both of you as soon as possible,' said Patrik. 'But right now I wonder if there's someone you'd like to phone. Or would you like us to contact the vicar here in Fjällbacka?'

As Patrik waited for a reply, Erica stepped forward to place her hand on the older sister's shoulder.

'Let's go have a coffee,' she said. Then she led both sisters back to their car. 'Give me the keys, and I'll drive.'

Five minutes later they were sitting in Josefina's café with a cup of strong, hot coffee in front of each of them.

'The neighbours rang us,' said the older sister, who now introduced herself as Tina. 'My husband and I have a summer house on the other side of town, and my sister just happened to be visiting. She's staying in our guest cottage.' She nodded at the younger woman, who was sitting silently beside her and staring down at her coffee cup. 'She was supposed to stay one week, but as usual she's mucked things up, so God only knows how long she'll be here.'

The younger sister looked at Erica. 'The person I rented a flat from came home earlier than expected. I'm doing my best to find another place to live.'

'I'm sorry, but I didn't catch your name,' said Erica, whose dislike for Tina, the older sister, was growing by the minute.

'Linnea,' said the woman quietly. She lifted her cup with trembling fingers.

'Is Mamma really dead?' she said. And now the tears spilled down her cheeks. 'I can't believe it.'

'I hardly think the police would lie about something like that,' snapped Tina as she got up to fetch more coffee.

She didn't ask Erica or her sister whether they'd care for a refill.

'Tell me about your mother,' said Erica.

'She had just realized her biggest dream,' said Linnea, slowly wiping away the tears with the back of her hand. 'Mamma has always loved clothes. She worked for years as a seamstress. She was such an expert; most of her customers belonged to the upper crust of Göteborg and she did a lot of alterations for the big, exclusive fashion houses. For years she dreamed of opening a small vintage clothing shop that would sell only the best – Dior, Chanel, Hermès, Louis Vuitton . . .'

'Your mother certainly had lovely things in her shop,' said Erica. 'But they weren't exactly cheap. I couldn't really understand how she was going to make ends meet here in Fjällbacka.'

'Precisely what I told her,' Tina said with a snort as she came back to join them at the table. 'It was the most idiotic idea I ever heard of! She might as well have tossed all of Pappa's money into the fireplace.'

'So what?' said Linnea. 'Pappa left the money to her. Why shouldn't she spend it on whatever she liked? Mamma wasn't stupid. She knew it was going to be a labour of love, and that the business

140

would never pay back what she put into it. That wasn't why she did it. She wasn't interested in making money. She wanted to have a house here in Fjällbacka, where she grew up, and a little shop on the ground floor filled with things that she loved. That's why Mamma opened the shop. To live her dream. Not to earn money.'

'But financially it was crazy!'

Tina's voice had risen to a falsetto.

'So what?' Linnea repeated. 'The money belonged to her.'

Tina shook her head and abruptly stood up. 'I refuse to sit here and listen to any more of this idiocy. Besides, we have important practical matters to attend to.'

Erica looked at Linnea's sad expression and saw that she was undoubtedly thinking the same thing. That it was too soon – their mother's body was hardly even cold.

'Probably one of the local drug addicts who thought there'd be cash in the till,' said Mellberg, scratching his scalp.

'Well, er, I'm not so sure about that,' said Patrik. He leaned down to pet Ernst. The dog was sitting next to his chair in the station's break room, begging with his head cocked to one side.

'No buns for you, my boy. Your mummy says you're getting too fat,' Mellberg said to the dog, who replied with a pitiful whine. 'Oh, what the hell. A few little buns aren't going to make anybody fat. Just look at me. I'm in great shape, and I eat at least two or three a day.'

Mellberg patted his huge paunch with satisfaction and then tossed a bun to Ernst. Patrik and Annika couldn't help exchanging an amused glance. If self-indulgence had been an Olympic sport, Mellberg would have won every gold medal going.

'I have a hard time imagining one of our local boys carrying out such a vicious assault. It seemed more . . . personal,' said Patrik.

'What do we know about the murder weapon?' asked Martin as he gave Ernst another bun.

None of them could resist Ernst's pleading brown eyes, and that was why the dog would soon be dragging his big belly along the ground.

'It's only been two days, so I haven't heard anything conclusive from the crime lab yet. It always takes a while, you know. But I asked if they could give me some idea, however vague, and unofficially of course. So they told me she'd been killed with something heavy that had sharp edges,' Patrik reported.

'Heavy with sharp edges. That could be lots of things,' said Mellberg gloomily. 'Any concrete evidence from the techs' examination of the shop?'

'No, nothing,' said Patrik. 'Any footprints were obliterated by the customers who came in and found her.'

'And nobody saw anyone coming out of the place? Seems strange. The perp must have had a car parked outside. And there's nothing missing from Lisbeth's private flat in the building?'

Martin reached for another bun and nodded when Annika asked if he'd like more coffee.

'The door to the flat upstairs was locked, so no one could have gone in. And the daughters report that nothing had been moved or taken. But . . .' And here Patrik hesitated. 'I'd still like to carry out a forensic examination of the flat.'

'Why?' asked Mellberg, looking cross. 'Why should we waste resources on that if no one got inside? As you must be aware, we're on a tight budget here.'

'Yes, I know. But I have a hunch . . . I'd also like to take a closer look at Lisbeth's finances, both her personal accounts and the shop's books.'

'This is going to be expensive. Especially given that it was probably a customer who broke in, and then things got out of control. But okay, go ahead – only this once, mind.'

Mellberg glared at Patrik, who heaved a sigh of relief. Apparently the chief was in a good mood today. Patrik got up and signalled with a nod for Martin to come with him. They had a lot to do.

'What are we going to do with all these things?' Linnea ran her hand lightly over the clothes displayed on hangers.

'I've already talked to the Once More shop in Göteborg. They've promised to buy everything,' said Tina. 'I just want to see if there are any goodies that I might want to have for myself.'

Her eyes sparkling, she reached for a long, sleek gown with a deep décolletage. It looked as if it belonged on the red carpet in Cannes.

'Dolce. How fabulous!'

She laid the dress aside and continued to rifle through the clothes, hanging some items back up but setting aside more until she had a huge pile of garments that she wanted to keep.

'Don't you want anything for yourself?' Tina laughed as she looked her sister up and down, taking in her sensible shoes and the nubby grey cardigan of no particular label.

'No,' said Linnea, embarrassed.

She'd never had any interest in clothes or fashion. Not like Tina. Or their mother.

'But we need to choose something for her to be buried in,' she quietly added, keeping her eyes fixed on the ground.

'I don't think it much matters what anyone wears once they're put in the ground,' replied Tina scornfully as she placed a chic patterned blouse on top of her pile of clothes.

'I realize that, but I'd still like Mamma to look nice.'

'For God's sake! OK, go ahead and choose something for Mamma. But check the price tag first so you don't take anything too expensive. No need to be extravagant.'

'All right,' said Linnea, her gaze still fixed on the toes of her shoes.

Tina's condescending manner had grown worse after the problems she'd encountered last winter. And the relationship between Lisbeth and her older daughter had deteriorated.

'Don't just stand there.' Tina pointed at the pile of clothing: 'Help me carry all these things out to the car.'

Linnea sighed and began gathering up the garments.

'I can't figure out what the motive could be,' said Patrik as he peeled yet another shrimp.

On the plate in front of him was an impressive heap of shrimp debris.

'But wasn't it a robbery?' said Anna, reaching for the bottle of white wine and refilling everyone's glass.

'Well, it's true that someone took the cash from the till, but according to Lisbeth's younger daughter there was never a lot of money in the shop.'

'What about the clothes? They must be worth quite a bit,' said Erica. She took a handful of shrimp from the big bowl in the middle of the table.

'Possibly, but it's not that easy to sell stolen goods. And I have a hard time picturing someone robbing a shop full of second-hand clothing.'

'Not second-hand, Patrik. Vintage.'

'Okay, okay. Vintage. But that doesn't seem like much of a motive.'

'Although the Chanel jacket that Lisbeth asked

me to look up might be worth around half a million kronor to the right buyer.'

Anna took a big bite of the shrimp sandwich she'd just made but instantly stopped chewing when she saw Erica and Patrik both staring at her.

'What? Didn't you know that? Lisbeth rang me up last week because she'd got in some clothing from an estate sale and found a jacket she suspected could be from Coco Chanel's very first collection. And that would make it super valuable. She knew that I have contacts at Sotheby's because of all the years I worked in the auction world. Her daughter Tina emailed me pictures of the jacket, and I checked it out for her. Didn't Tina tell you?'

Anna finished chewing and swallowed her food. Patrik was shaking his head.

'No, she didn't say a word about that. And I just found out that she's in a real bind because an audit around Christmastime revealed that over half a million kronor has gone missing from the company where she works. It's currently under investigation, but they're fairly certain that Tina was the one who embezzled the money by issuing fake invoices. So tell me more about this jacket.'

'Well, I sent out the photos, and of course they'll need to see the jacket in person before they can make a definite determination. But apparently it looks to be genuine. And the price depends a bit on finding the right buyer, but several collectors have expressed interest, and they'll be taking bids, so . . . half a million is not far off.'

'For a jacket? Good Lord. That's absurd.' Patrik shook his head.

'Oh, right. That's equivalent to the big toe of some star football player like Zlatan when he gets sold to a team,' Anna mocked. 'And that's a much more sensible way of spending the money.'

'You can't compare the two things,' replied Patrik. 'Zlatan is . . . er . . . Oh, it's no use trying to explain to anyone who has no interest in sports, like the two of you.'

'I'm on your side, Patrik. I'd much rather buy a piece of Zlatan than a Chanel jacket.' Erica grinned.

'In that case, I know which piece I'd buy,' Anna said with a big smile.

'Good Lord. You guys are hopeless. But thanks for your help, Anna. This gives us something to work with in the morning. Plus we've been given a warrant to search Lisbeth's flat above the shop.'

'And Lisbeth's funeral is tomorrow,' said Erica, picturing the sorrow she'd seen in Linnea's eyes.

Gusts of cold springtime wind swept across the Fjällbacka cemetery. The mourners who had gathered for the burial stood with their backs to the church, which loomed like a mighty granite tower over the small village. Not an especially large group of people, as Tina noted. And no wonder. Her mother had been an ordinary person who lived an ordinary life. The one redeeming feature had been her encyclopedic knowledge of fashion. That was the only point at which Tina's world connected with her mother's.

And in the end it had also proved to be Tina's lifeline. She knew that she would be forced to pay back all the money that she'd borrowed from the company. Half a million kronor – that was a lot of money. She had never intended to take such a large sum. At first she'd taken only small amounts. Enough to be able to buy herself a few nice things. A pair of black Louboutins. A blouse from Chloé. An Hermès scarf. Marvellous little things that had made life worth living. Then suddenly the sum had grown so large that she couldn't possibly pay it back. So she had placed all her hopes on her mother. Lisbeth had inherited three million from their father, after all, and some of the money really belonged to Tina. Instead Lisbeth had used the funds to realize her ridiculous dream. She might as well have burned it in the woodstove. And then there was that jacket. When Lisbeth asked her daughter for help in having it appraised, Tina knew at once that this could be her ticket out of the financial straits in which she'd landed. Half a million kronor. It would have solved all her problems. She had begged and pleaded, but her mother stubbornly shook her head as she kept on repeating the same old lines. She told Tina that she needed to take responsibility for her own life, that she couldn't depend on other people to solve her problems. The same crap that she'd always had to put up with. All of a sudden it was as if her brain short-circuited and rage took over. She'd picked up an iron and struck again and again until Lisbeth was no longer breathing.

She realized it was only a matter of time before she was caught. The police were going to search her mother's flat today. There they'd find traces from when she went upstairs to clean herself up afterwards and wash off all the blood. So she had a plan. She'd booked a plane ticket. As soon as she'd picked up the jacket she would drive straight to the airport. Then it would just be a matter of finding some way to sell it. Combined with the money she'd taken from her husband's account, she would have a nice little sum to start a new life.

Tina had to hold back a smile. People were so stupid, so weak. And her own family was the worst. Especially Linnea, standing there weeping as their mother's coffin was lowered into the ground.

'What did you choose for her to wear?' Tina asked, in an effort to distract Linnea and stop her crying.

'I didn't take anything from the shop – I was afraid of choosing something too expensive,' said Linnea, in between sobs. 'But I had a pair of black trousers from H&M that I once borrowed from Mamma and didn't have a chance to return. And an old black jacket that I found in a carrier bag in the kitchen.'

Tina stared at her sister, then slowly shifted her gaze to look down at the coffin.

DREAMING OF ELISABETH

The sound of the waves lapping against the boat were lulling her to sleep. The gentle rocking motion, the murmuring voices from the other boats, the heat that was making beads of sweat form in the small of her back – all of it was compelling her to sink into that borderland just before sleep took over. It was a place that she had begun to dread. But her limbs felt so heavy and hot that she didn't have the strength to stop herself from sliding into the unconscious state, into memory. Inevitably, the images came flooding in. Red against white. The blood on the tiles. Memories that made her heart ache. Her brain screamed at her muscles to move, to do something, anything, to rouse her from that endless loop into which she was now being forced.

'Malin, dinner is ready.'

With a feeling of relief, she gave a start and then sat up. The boat careened and she instinctively grabbed hold of the lifeline that ran around the perimeter.

'Food's ready!'

Lars climbed up out of the galley. For a second she considered telling him about the images, about what was constantly preventing her from getting enough sleep. But she resisted the impulse. It wouldn't do any good. There had been a time when she'd thought they could talk to each other, but she no longer had any such illusions.

She studied Lars as she took a bite of the Caesar salad he'd prepared for both of them.

'Who was on the phone earlier?' she asked.

'Nobody.'

Lars waved his hand dismissively but refused to look her in the eye.

'Well, someone must have been.'

For a moment neither of them spoke.

'It was only the office,' he said at last.

'Don't they know you're on holiday?'

She knew she ought to stop now. It wouldn't serve any purpose, and he'd just get annoyed. But she couldn't help herself.

'You said you would take some time off. No work allowed on this holiday.'

Malin cursed her nagging tone of voice, but anger and frustration robbed her of all common sense, leaving in their wake a disappointed child.

'They needed to consult me about a patient. It only took ten minutes. And besides, you were asleep.'

Lars tossed down his fork and gazed out at the

sea. After a moment he picked it up again, and they resumed eating, though the silence was so heavy with all that was not being said that they might as well have been screaming at each other.

'I'm going for a walk,' Lars finally announced after they'd finished eating.

'Go ahead. I'll do the dishes.'

She stared after him as he took off along the dock.

Three days later they were headed north towards a different harbour. They'd been sailing for nearly ten days, and by now the boat was overloaded with unfulfilled expectations. Maybe it had been naive to think that everything would work itself out if they simply bought a sailboat and took a month-long holiday. Thinking they could leave everything behind and let the wind blow away the memories.

The boat had been her idea. She had practically grown up on a sailboat, and Lars had owned boats for years before they'd met. But because of what had happened to his first wife, Malin had hesitated for a long time before voicing her suggestion. To her surprise, Lars had been enthusiastic, calling it an 'excellent idea'. So they had bought the boat. A real beauty in the five-million-kronor class with every comfort imaginable. Malin could have settled for something less pretentious, but she'd let Lars have his way. The money that she'd inherited from her paternal grandfather wasn't doing anybody any good just sitting in the bank.

If the funds could give them a new start, it would be money well spent.

'Here, I've made coffee.' Lars came up beside Malin as she stood in the bow. They were out on open water, with no other boats in sight and only a few islands nearby. The wind had picked up, and the bow was bucking against the waves.

'Thanks.' Malin took the cup but kept her gaze on the sea. The boat was on autopilot. Lars was still standing next to her.

'Malin . . .' he began hesitantly.

She didn't turn to face him, merely waited tensely for him to go on.

'Malin . . .' he repeated. He seemed to be having trouble working out what he wanted to say. She waited.

'I . . .'

A deep trough in the swells surprised both of them, and the boat abruptly pitched downward. Malin lost her footing. As she was tossed towards the guard rail, she felt Lars's hand on her back. For a brief moment she thought he was trying to give her a push, shove her over the rail and down into the foaming sea. Then she felt his fingers grabbing her jacket and pulling her back. She turned around.

'That was close,' said Lars. She saw a flicker of emotion in his eyes. Then he spun on his heel and went back to the cockpit.

There was nothing the matter with her. One doctor after another had told her as much. They simply couldn't find anything physically wrong. No one could explain why the babies refused to stay inside of her. No one could explain the blood that flowed out with such merciless regularity. Three months. That was the longest she'd been able to carry a foetus. Then the blood had stained the tiles red in the bathroom, and she had wept tears of resignation and despair.

In the beginning Lars had stood by her. Comforting her, encouraging her, ensuring that she stayed calm, reminding her to take her vitamins. He had protected her. But each time she lost a baby, lost his baby, he'd retreated more and more. Until she had come to view this holiday as their last chance.

What a joke! Nothing on this trip had turned out as she had imagined.

She nodded to a couple in a nearby boat. They were docked in the visitors' marina in Grebbestad, crowded together with thousands of other boat owners. She hated it. The place felt claustrophobic. But Lars had told her that he had things to do, which made it necessary to spend a few days near a town. Malin couldn't bring herself to ask him what was so important. Probably something to do with his job. As usual. He was a doctor, which provided him with an excellent excuse to escape whenever the mood at home got too sad, too gloomy. Today's errand had kept him away for three hours, taking care of some business or other.

He looked stressed when he finally came walking back towards the boat. Malin watched his lean figure approach, moving with that typical sauntering gait of his. She still found him tremendously attractive. It hadn't taken her more than a few minutes to fall for him five years ago when they met for the first time at a party hosted by a mutual acquaintance. His hair was starting to go grey at the temples, but that was the only indication that he'd reached the age of forty-five. She herself was about to turn forty. Forty years old and childless. She bit her knuckle to prevent the tears from flowing again.

'Hi.'

He came aboard without meeting her eye.

'Hi.'

Malin began feverishly draping the newly washed laundry over the guard rail. She tried hard not to ask any questions, but the effort proved too much for her.

'You were gone a long time.'

'Mmm . . .'

Lars went below decks into the cabin. He still hadn't looked at her.

'What were you doing?'

She raised her voice to be heard, but the only reply was the sound of clanking pots and pans. Half an hour later the food was ready. She was still brimming with questions, but the wall between them was so insurmountable that she didn't think he'd listen to her queries. Instead they talked about trivial topics. What the weather forecaster had said. How many boats were moored in the harbour. How loud the music was on that boat crowded with young people only a short distance away. Nothing of importance. Just letters arranged into words, incapable of tearing down any walls or providing answers to anything significant. Merely air, breathed in and out.

Towards the end of the meal, Malin noticed a dull ache starting up in her stomach. The pain caused the memories to explode in fireworks of images. It was as if the babies hadn't spilled out of her, one after another, but instead had gathered inside of her. She threw herself at the rail and vomited. Then everything went black.

She had been ill for two days, Lars told her. When she awoke, the dreams were still vivid in her mind. Those horrible, feverish dreams, as clear as if she'd seen them in a film. Pictures of Lars's first wife, Elisabeth, whom she'd seen only in photos. They had never met. Elisabeth had fallen overboard when a bad storm took her and Lars by surprise as they were sailing in the Mediterranean. Lars had never wanted to talk about it, but out of curiosity Malin had looked up the newspaper articles describing what had happened.

Those grainy photos in the paper hadn't done Lars justice. They showed him after he'd come ashore in a storm-damaged boat. Without Elisabeth. And there were pictures of him at the funeral service, his face haggard as his wife was remembered by family and friends.

Her body was never found. She'd fallen overboard and disappeared. For ever.

But now Malin had seen her. In her dreams, Elisabeth had tumbled over the rail, backwards, while looking straight at Malin, who could clearly see her lips moving. She had desperately tried to work out what Elisabeth was saying. At first she seemed to be saying: 'Save me.' But then Malin thought the words she uttered before falling into the sea and vanishing for ever were: 'Save yourself!'

She opened her mouth to tell Lars, but changed her mind. In the end, she said nothing. But when sleep returned, she once again saw Elisabeth's face.

As soon as Malin was back on her feet, they left Grebbestad. Until that point, Lars had been the one who usually took the helm, but now that they were headed out of the harbour using the motor, Malin insisted on steering. A short time later they set the sails, and as they billowed in the wind, she felt the past few days being washed out of her mind. She was about to ask Lars to sheet home a bit when he did just that. Malin smiled. At least as sailors they made a good team.

Lars seemed to be simmering with suppressed anticipation. He radiated a tense energy even though he was doing his best to appear impassive.

That worried her. The dreams about Elisabeth had been so real. So insistent. As if trying to tell her something. As if Elisabeth wanted to tell her something.

'Looks like a storm's brewing.'

Malin flinched. She'd been so lost in her own thoughts that she hadn't noticed Lars come to the cockpit to stand beside her. She followed his gaze and peered at the horizon. He was right. Huge black clouds had formed, and the wind was gathering force. The big sailboat was now racing forward through foaming swells that slapped against the bow.

'Didn't you listen to the weather report this morning?' Malin asked, glancing at Lars. 'I thought you said we would have clear skies with a light wind.'

He ran his hand through his hair, looking annoyed. She knew that gesture of his so well.

'No, I didn't say that. I assumed you had listened to the forecast. You were the one who insisted on being the skipper today.'

Malin didn't reply. It was no use arguing over what either of them had said or done. No matter what, the weather was getting worse, and they had no option but to deal with it.

'Release the mainsail,' she said as the boat began tilting even more. She had to brace one foot against the side of the cockpit to keep her balance. 'Maybe we should turn back,' she added nervously, looking at Lars.

He shook his head. 'Absolutely not. We need to get to Strömstad today.'

Malin was surprised by his strong reaction.

'Why? Why do we need to get to Strömstad?'

'We just do.'

'But—'

She was about to protest, but he turned away.

'Keep sailing, goddammit!' he shouted, making Malin jump.

Her uneasiness, which had been growing stronger over the past weeks, now erupted full force. She hardly recognized him. All those secrets he'd been keeping, all those little excursions when he'd gone off alone, all those mysterious phone calls. Her anxiety now merged with images of Elisabeth. Malin pictured her predecessor on a sailboat with heavy clouds overhead and strong winds battling to take control of the boat. Images of her in the water. Underwater. Silently drifting with her long hair floating around her face. And her dead eyes.

Feeling her heart turn to ice, Malin studied Lars's back as he went to release the sail. She suddenly felt that she was watching a stranger. She tried to conjure up memories from the past, from the years they'd spent together. But the only thing she saw when she looked back was the blood on the tiles. The feeling of life running out of her. The sympathetic and tender look that she'd seen on Lars's face as he held her after each miscarriage now seemed, after the fact, to have been nothing

160

more than a mask. As if he'd been someone else. As if he were feeling something else behind that sorrowful persona. Why hadn't the doctors ever been able to find anything wrong with her? Why couldn't they explain why she couldn't keep a baby alive in her womb?

The wind was blowing harder, and Malin was getting scared. She was an experienced sailor, but she'd never been out in a storm like this. Why had Lars insisted that they keep going?

She was suddenly so certain of his motive that she almost collapsed. Somehow she forced herself to take a firmer grip on the wheel, staring into the storm as pieces of the puzzle fell into place, one by one. His hand pressed against her back as she stumbled – he could as easily have pushed her overboard as pulled her to safety. And that bout of what Lars had said was food poisoning, during which she'd slipped in and out of consciousness. In and out of Elisabeth's world. And now. The fact that he claimed she was the one who had checked the weather forecast. Today they were going to end up in the middle of a storm, just as Elisabeth had six years earlier. And yet he had insisted that they carry on, straight into the bad weather.

Malin began shaking uncontrollably. Everything was suddenly crystal clear. This was what Elisabeth had tried to warn her about in the dream. 'Save yourself!' That was what she had said before she fell over the side. Pushed by Lars. Malin now had no doubt that it must have happened that way. Everything fit. And after she was gone, Lars would once again play the role of the grieving widower. A widower who would inherit a considerable fortune from his late wife. It was all so banal. So incredibly banal.

Malin glanced at her husband, who was struggling with the sail, and then she made up her mind. She would heed the warning that Elisabeth had delivered in those feverish dreams. She would save herself, no matter what the cost. She had no intention of becoming Lars's next victim.

With great determination she swung the rudder to port and struck. The boom came flying with tremendous force, and Lars just managed to duck in time. He turned around with an expression that showed both surprise and anger.

'What the hell are you doing?' he shouted over the roaring of the squalls.

Malin didn't reply. She kept on turning the boat. Lars was coming towards her. Water sprayed over the boat and into his face. Malin realized that she too was getting drenched. But she no longer felt anything. She was completely empty inside. Cold. The way she was every time a child left her body.

By the time Lars got closer, she had swung the boat all the way around and the wind once again filled the sails. In her mind, the film was playing over and over – the sequence where Elisabeth fell overboard. The look of surprise on her face, changing to fear. Then her lips shaping those same words over and over again: 'Save yourself, save yourself, save . . . your . . .'

Lars hopped down next to Malin and grabbed her arm. Hard. Desperately she tried to pull away, her fear growing worse with every second.

'What are you doing?' he shouted in her ear. But she was so terrified that she couldn't answer. Instead, she yanked her arm out of his grasp and ran. She made it up three steps to the deck before Lars caught her and again grabbed her by the arm.

'Calm down! What's wrong with you?'

Panic was making her pulse race. She knew it was only a matter of seconds before she would follow Elisabeth down into the deep. A sense of resignation made her close her eyes tight and wait for the inevitable. There was nothing more she could do.

At that moment the boat careened in protest because no one was standing at the wheel, and again the boom came flying. This time Lars didn't manage to duck. With a horrible crunch the boom struck him on the back of the head. Malin flung herself out of the way as he flew past her and over the guard rail. For a few seconds he fumbled for something to grab. She saw his outstretched hand, the panic in his eyes, and knew that she had a choice to make. As if it was no longer attached to her, she found her hand automatically reaching out for his. Only a centimetre separated their fingers when she again heard Elisabeth's voice in her head.

She pulled her hand back.

Her fingers trembled on the wheel. In the distance she saw Grebbestad harbour, only ten minutes away. It was tempting to turn back. But she realized if she did that, no one would believe her when she said that Lars had fallen overboard in the fierce storm. Reluctantly she went about. The wind was whipping up huge swells behind her. For a moment she thought she caught a glimpse of Lars in the waves. That was the deciding factor. She turned the wheel and the boat responded reluctantly as it again headed in the direction of Strömstad. The storm scared her, but Elisabeth's voice urged her on. She wasn't doing this only to save herself. She was also doing this for Elisabeth.

After a terrifying journey she finally caught sight of Strömstad harbour. In her mind she rehearsed over and over what she would do. And say. She didn't have to pretend to be upset. The adrenalin that had surged through her body had begun to ease, leaving her in a trembling state, shivering and sobbing. It took all the resolve she could muster to pull into a visitor's berth at one of the docks. Exhausted, she collapsed in the cockpit, shuddering as she lay on the floorboards. Again and again she went over what had happened. Bitterness left a sour taste in her mouth, but otherwise she felt completely dead inside. She didn't feel the water that soaked through her clothes all the way to her skin. It had nothing to do with her. All her senses seemed to have stopped functioning. She felt nothing. Absolutely nothing. But she had no doubt whatsoever that she'd had no choice but to do what she did. One of them was not coming back alive from that sailing trip. And it turned out to be Lars. Not her.

'Malin?'

A voice forced its way through the haze of exhaustion in her brain. At first she thought it was Elisabeth's voice she was hearing, yet it sounded more familiar. Confused, Malin raised her head and tried to focus. She thought she'd heard someone say her name, but that was impossible. She dismissed the notion.

'Malin!'

Now she was seeing more clearly she could make out a group of people standing on the dock. And someone was definitely saying her name.

'Yvonne?' said Malin. She found herself looking up at her best friend. But wasn't she in Stockholm? Thoughts swirled through her mind. Nothing made any sense. For a moment she wondered if all the stress was making her hallucinate. But Yvonne was not the only person she recognized. She saw her sister Lotta, three of her colleagues, and a handful of other friends. With a great effort Malin sat up and peered at the faces of so many of the people that she loved. They looked worried, surprised.

'Where's Lars? That was a terrible storm you came through. We rang Lars before you left Grebbestad and told him we could go over there instead. But he'd put so much work into making plans for your surprise fortieth birthday party, and he's rented a banquet room here in Strömstad, so . . .'

Yvonne's voice faded as she looked at the boat in bewilderment.

Malin felt herself slowly slip away. She was again dreaming about Elisabeth. But this time Lars was at Elisabeth's side.

THE WIDOWS' CAFÉ

The buns were arranged on platters. The biscuits were in fancy glass jars next to the cash register, and the satin steel of the brand-new espresso machine gleamed behind her. Marianne walked around to the front of the counter and took a couple of steps back to admire her creation. She'd done the exact same thing every morning since opening the Widows' Café almost three years ago. Sometimes she found everything to her satisfaction. But sometimes she didn't. Today she wasn't entirely pleased with the way the glass of the display had been polished. Inside were the newly made open-face sandwiches, piled high with ham, cheese, roast beef, or shrimp. With a few expert swipes of a dishcloth, she polished the glass so it sparkled in the sun coming through the windows at the front of the shop. She could see her own face reflected in the glass. That round face, which had provoked so many sighs of dissatisfaction from her when she was young. These days she found it perfectly suited to her grey hair, still so thick and lovely as it framed her round face.

It was the location that had made her fall for this place. She'd been thinking about opening a café for ages, but her dream had never materialized because she couldn't find the right premises. By chance she had come across the old village shop when she was out taking one of her long walks, and for some reason she couldn't get the place out of her mind. Every little crack, every shabby detail of the building had become etched into her memory. Not that she had paid much attention to how shabby it looked. Instead, she'd seen the potential that was underneath. Now that potential had been realized. She'd put all the money that Ruben had left her into the renovation work, and it had been worth every öre. Best money she ever spent, as the Americans would say. And that was honestly how she felt.

Someone was trying to open the door, so Marianne went over to let in the first customers of the morning. The Widows' Café was ready to greet the day.

'Are you lying to me?'
His voice has that tone that makes her instinctively flinch and crouch down, trying to make herself as small as possible. But usually it doesn't help. He takes a step forward. Now he raises his hand. She looks at the palm of his hand, seeing the lifeline and the heartline. Parallel,

and yet intertwined. Then the blow falls. First the sound.
That sharp, resounding slap. Then the pain. The burning
sensation. And finally darkness.

'Where would you like to sit?'

The bright voice made Marianne look up and study the couple who had just come in. The woman was thin and petite, her eyes flitting around nervously. The man was big, with a presence that felt like an intrusive and unwelcome guest.

'Where do I usually want to sit?' he said in a tone of voice that made the woman cringe.

'Near the window,' she said timidly as she led him over to a window table a few metres away. She cast a glance at Marianne, who hastened to smile in her direction. The woman looked as if she could use a good supply of smiles.

'Just coffee for me,' said the man, taking the seat with the best view of the sea, which was only a short distance away. Frowning with annoyance, he stared out of the window, as if the world outside was standing by to attack him. Then he turned to look at the woman, who was heading towards Marianne.

'And make sure it's strong. I don't want any of that tepid dishwater like we got at the café in town.'

The woman merely nodded.

'Two coffees,' she said, staring at her hands, which were clutching her purse so tightly that her knuckles were white.

'Would you care for a bun with your coffee?' Marianne reached for the platter. 'It's on the house. You look as though you could use a little meat on your bones.'

The woman looked at the buns and seemed to hesitate. Then she glanced over her shoulder at the man sitting at the table and firmly shook her head.

'No. No, thank you. He doesn't like . . .' Again she shook her head, allowing the rest of her sentence to fade away. Her blonde hair fell softly over her shoulders, and Marianne could see tiny scars on her face. Spidery little lines where the skin had split open and then healed.

'But I'd like a Widow's Special, please.'

Marianne gave her a searching look. 'Are you sure, sweetie?'

She didn't take her eyes off the young woman. For a moment, thousands of unspoken questions seemed to hover in the air, but they vanished as the woman slowly nodded.

'Then that's what you shall have,' said Marianne, turning her back to her customer to fill the order with her usual efficiency.

When the couple left half an hour later, she quickly cleared their table and went into the kitchen to wash the cups. When you ran your own business, you had to be very careful.

'You're fucking useless! Do you hear me? I could crush you and not even break into a sweat. Do you realize that?'

He tightens his grip on her arm. Hatred and rage pour out of him. As if there's something dark, something hollow inside of him. A hidden spot where all the hate and anger is stored – until it boils over because she doesn't measure up, doesn't do as he says. Fails to be the person she ought to be.

'Why the hell should I keep you around if you can't even clean things properly? Look at this! Do you see that? Do you?'

He twists her arm into an awkward position as he forces her down on the floor. With his free hand he presses her face against the kitchen floor, right in front of the cooker.

'Do you see it? Do you see it now? Is that how it's supposed to look?'

She looks as best she can with his fingers painfully gripping the back of her neck. But she doesn't see a thing. The floor is gleaming after she scrubbed it for the second time today. It's so spotless that she can see her own reflection in the wood. Not that it matters what she sees. Or doesn't see. Because he sees something, so something must be there. She no longer asks any questions.

The girl who sometimes helped out in the café had just gone home when the bell above the door rang.

'We're closed,' said Marianne, without looking up.

She was adding up the cash in the till, and she didn't want to lose count.

'I'm not here as a customer,' said a voice, and when Marianne raised her eyes, at first all she saw was something shiny. Her glasses were perched on the tip of her nose, so she pushed them back up and realized the shiny object was a police badge.

'I'm from the police. Detective Inspector Eva Wärn.'

'The police?' said Marianne, raising one eyebrow. 'What's this about? Don't tell me one of the customers who was here when the boy swiped a couple of buns has bothered to report the theft. The kid looked so hungry, I don't begrudge him a single crumb. I would have given him the buns for free, if he'd asked.'

Eva Wärn waved her hand dismissively. 'This is about a more serious matter.'

The inspector nodded towards a table near the cash register. 'Could we sit down for a moment?'

'Sure. Of course. But can I offer you some coffee, since we're going to sit down anyway? I've just bought this amazing machine, so I can have two cups ready in a matter of minutes.'

Marianne tenderly patted her espresso machine, which had quickly become an invaluable addition to the café.

'Well . . .' Eva Wärn hesitated, but the thought of drinking something other than the wretched police station brew seemed to defeat her instinct to decline, and she nodded brusquely. 'All right.

Thanks. I suppose one cup wouldn't hurt. Could you make it a caffe latte?'

'Certainly, my dear,' replied Marianne, and she turned around to begin fiddling with the apparatus. After the machine had steamed and sputtered for a few moments, she placed a latte on the table in front of the officer, with a dusting of cinnamon on top of the white foam.

'There you are. Now we're ready to have a proper conversation,' said Marianne with satisfaction. 'So what's this all about?'

Eva sipped her coffee, seemingly reluctant to broach the reason for her visit. But when the silence began to feel oppressive, she said:

'We've discovered a rather odd coincidence.'

Marianne leaned forward with interest.

'An odd coincidence? That sounds exciting.'

Eva gave her a stern look.

'There have been a number of strange deaths lately. At first there didn't seem to be any connection between them, because they occurred both in our own police district and in other areas. But when we noticed the coincidence . . .'

She took another sip of coffee, refusing to look Marianne in the eye.

Marianne didn't say a word. Instead, she leaned back, calmly regarding the woman sitting across from her. After a lengthy silence, the inspector went on:

'In the past three years, four men have died mysteriously. The youngest was twenty-five, the oldest fifty-three. Without warning, they simply collapsed, and for lack of any other explanation, the pathologist has blamed their deaths on heart problems.'

'I see. But then what's the problem? It's not uncommon for men to die from a heart attack, and four men in three years . . .' Marianne left her sentence hanging as she threw out her hands.

The detective inspector meditatively stirred her coffee with a spoon as she focused all her attention on the foam in the glass. That gave Marianne the opportunity to study the woman in more detail. She had a tired look about her. She seemed to be about forty, but in the bright sunlight coming in through the big shop windows, she looked older. Her dark hair was cut in a page-boy style that was practical but not particularly attractive. And a few strands of grey were visible here and there. Apparently she wasn't sufficiently vain to colour her hair.

Eva Wärn raised her eyes from her glass to look Marianne straight in the eye.

'You're right.' She paused and then went on. 'It's not unusual for men to die from a heart attack. But what's odd is that all of them seem to have called in here for a coffee before they died. Since the cause of death was rather uncertain in each case, the wives were interviewed and asked to describe what they had done the day before their husbands passed away. I've read the reports from those interviews, and in every case, the Widows'

Café was mentioned. That's rather odd. Don't you agree?'

Her expression was cold and hard, but Marianne merely smiled.

'Strange coincidences happen all the time.' Her eyes sparkled with mischief as she added: 'Maybe it was my delicious buns that made their arteries clog up.'

'I can assure you that I don't find this the least bit funny.'

'No. Of course not,' said Marianne, in a serious tone of voice. But the sparkle in her eyes was still there.

'I don't know what you want me to say,' she went on, again throwing out her hands. 'The men came here to have coffee with their wives, and then had the misfortune to die of a heart attack. There's not much I can do about that.'

'That's not the only thing these men had in common.' Not for a second did Eva Wärn take her eyes off Marianne. 'They were all known to beat their wives.'

'Oh, that's awful. There are some very unpleasant men out there.'

Marianne reached for a bun from the platter on the counter and, with a look of contentment, she took a big bite.

'Are you sure you won't have one? It's on the house.'

'No, thanks,' said the inspector curtly, looking as if the mere idea was repulsive. Then she abruptly stood up. 'It appears we're not going to get anywhere with this.'

'Feel free to come back,' said Marianne cheerfully as she too stood up, brushing the sugar from her fingertips.

Eva Wärn didn't reply. The shop bell rang as she slammed the door behind her.

'Where have you been? It can't take an hour to shop for groceries!'

His voice is shrill.

'There were a lot of people in the shop. Tomorrow is Midsummer's Eve, you know. Everybody wanted to . . .' She can hear the panic in her voice. The queues were so long. She had shifted from one foot to another, looking at her watch every minute, knowing that she would be in trouble when she got home.

Wham! His arm connects with her cheekbone. For a moment she wonders how hard a blow a cheekbone can withstand before it shatters like a hollow stick. But this time it holds. She feels only the mute, burning sting on her skin.

'Who were you meeting? You might as well tell me! Who have you been meeting behind my back? Answer me!'

He's shouting so loudly that the neighbours will soon start to complain. And she knows what will happen then. The police will arrive and knock on the door. He will go to open it. Courteous, well-mannered. He'll explain that his wife is temperamental and occasionally raises her voice more than necessary. It's nothing – a minor disagreement, that's all. But thanks for coming over, officers. And then they will leave. And she will have to bear the brunt of his rage at being humiliated.

She surrenders. As she invariably does. Offers no protests. Does not defend herself. Simply accepts whatever he doles out.

The hot summer air struck Eva like a wall. Her uniform was always too heavy for the summer weather. She could feel drops of sweat rolling down her back. What a strange encounter that was at the Widows' Café. Such a calm and peaceful setting. The café's owner, with her grey hair, her glasses perched on the tip of her nose, and her gentle smile – the woman reminded her of her beloved grandmother. There was something so maternal about her, so warm, that Eva had struggled to resist the urge to lean her head against the woman's voluminous bosom and breathe in the scent of flour and cinnamon.

A tear spilled down her cheek, and she wiped it away with annoyance. So undignified. So pathetic. Why was she allowing this interview to have such an effect on her? Yet she'd known in advance that it would do just that. It was sheer chance that she'd stumbled upon the connection to the Widows' Café after reading through the reports, but she had realized immediately that this was a turning point. Before she even set foot in the café the whispers had reached her. Like a muted murmuring, the rumours had come and gone over the years. No one had wanted to say anything to her; they saw her as an outsider, an enemy. What they didn't know was that she was one of them. That was a secret nobody knew.

She got in the police car and tried to pull herself together. It was time to go back to the station. None of her colleagues had any idea what she was working on. She'd told no one about the link that she'd discovered. No one knew about the Widows' Café. And that was exactly the way she wanted it. Now she just needed time to think.

By the end of summer Marianne had almost forgotten about the inspector's visit to her café. Occasionally their conversation would pop up in her mind though. Not because it had been unpleasant – she'd been through too much in her life to find anything particularly unpleasant any more. No, it was because of the vulnerability she'd seen emanating from the police officer beneath that tough facade. That was what continued to nag at her thoughts.

The moment she saw the couple come through the door, that memory rose to the surface again. She'd never seen them before. They were not among her steady customers. She happened to have a photographic memory for faces, and she could recall everyone who had ever entered the café. Yet she knew at once. She felt an immediate sisterhood. A connection, like an invisible bond, between her and the woman. There was something in their eyes that always gave them away. A hunted look. Panic hovering just out of sight.

She watched the couple as they sat down at a table in the corner. The man looked deceptively meek. Short, grey, insignificant. All the same, there was something in his eyes that she recognized all too well. He had Ruben's eyes. Part hatred, part unreasonable anger, part aggression, and part malice. She knew the recipe by heart.

The woman looked in her direction and their eyes locked. Marianne's heart ached. She could feel the woman's pain as clearly as if it were her own. In fact, it was almost worse to sense another person's troubles. Marianne's pain was over. She had confronted it. Confronted the fear. At last.

The woman came over to her.

It had taken almost half an hour to get home. Kjell could feel the anger smouldering and sputtering inside him. An hour wasted on going out for a fucking cup of coffee. Beata had been going on about it for weeks, until he'd eventually given in and agreed to go with her. Although afterwards he couldn't understand why. The café was nothing special. It was in a good location, of course, but there was nothing to set it apart from all the other coffee shops in the city. They could have gone somewhere local and been home in five minutes. Still, the coffee was excellent; that much he had to admit. Strong, hot, and with a slight taste of something . . . different. Some sort of spice. Maybe cardamom.

'Well, are you satisfied now?'

Kjell slammed the car door, gleefully noting how Beata flinched.

'Finally you can stop nagging me about taking you to that place, right? I can't for the life of me understand why we had to go there. And now Sunday's almost over. Do you realize how much I could have got done in the time we spent on this? Do you?'

He pushed Beata through the door ahead of him. The anger inside him was growing with every word, and he could hardly wait to let it loose. The sense of relief afterwards was always so enormous, so liberating. All the tension evaporated, and for a while he could breathe easier. Sometimes he'd be filled with a vague sense of regret, but over the years he'd taught himself to repress that feeling.

'How could you dream up something so stupid! Don't you think I have better things to do than sit around and guzzle coffee on the weekend?'

He grabbed her hair and pulled her head backwards. But much to his surprise he didn't see the usual look of submission and resignation. Instead he saw something that resembled . . . no, how could that be possible? Was that triumph in her eyes?

Kjell raised his hand to strike, determined to pound that sudden, disrespectful look out of Beata's eyes. But an acute twinge of pain forced him to drop his hand. He pressed it to his chest. The pain seemed to rip and claw at the area around his heart. Unaware of what he was doing, his other hand let go of Beata's hair, and she collapsed in a heap at his feet. There she stayed.

Watching, observing. And as the pain intensified and he felt the floor rise up to meet him, he once again saw that look of triumph on her face.

Ruben hadn't been like that in the beginning. He had been a quiet man, considerate, almost shy. That was what had attracted her. Having grown up with four rowdy brothers, she had truly appreciated Ruben's gentleness when he was courting her.

It didn't take more than two days after their wedding for his anger to come pouring out. The anger that seemed to boil and seethe inside him, always on the alert for mistakes, an excuse to spew out its hateful lava. She no longer remembered what had caused the first explosion, which was far from the last of his outbursts. Maybe it was something important. Maybe it was something minor. That had ceased to matter.

For twenty years she put up with it. Twenty years that had marked her body, her soul, her heart for all eternity. When at last she put a stop to it, she was surprised to discover how easy it was. How weak Ruben actually was. Her experience as a nurse had provided the answer. Sometimes she cursed her stupidity. Why hadn't she decided sooner to do what had to be done? It turned out to be so easy.

The only way she could forgive herself for not putting her foot down earlier was by passing her experience on. She knew how to do it. How easy it was. Rumours had quickly spread in the covert network that existed. The secret network that protected those women who had no other way out.

And so they came to her. Not many, but a few. More than that police detective knew.

They had all come to the Widows' Café.

Autumn leaves swirled past the windows. Business had been extraordinarily good all summer, with a steady stream of new customers. Now, on the verge of autumn, only the regular customers were left. Those who always chose the same tables, always ordered the same type of coffee and pastry. Those who thrived on familiar routines and settings, and who saw Marianne and her café as a refuge from their daily chores. This was the time of year that Marianne liked best. When the café was quiet and calm, and her guests had to speak in low voices unless they wanted everyone else to hear their conversations. When the sound of a teaspoon striking a china platter sounded like a gunshot and made all the other customers jump. The summer season was essential if the café was going to stay in business, but this was the time when she found peace of mind.

Pling. The bell over the door announced a new customer. Marianne was squatting down behind the counter taking inventory of the coffee on hand, so she had to stand up to see who had come in.

'Hello.'

With a stern nod, Detective Inspector Eva Wärn greeted Marianne.

'Hello,' replied Marianne, regarding the inspector and her companion with interest.

This time she saw two police officers. Eva Wärn and a male colleague. Both were in uniform, both wore expressions that were equally grim.

'How can I help the city authorities today?' said Marianne with a smile.

Eva Wärn cast a fleeting glance at her colleague.

'You know what I want,' he said brusquely. Then he went over to the table next to the window and sat down with his back to Marianne.

The female inspector hesitantly approached the counter. She avoided looking Marianne in the eye. Instead, she studied the selection of cakes in the display case.

'Are you on duty today?' asked Marianne, but the officer didn't answer. Eva Wärn continued to study the baked goods as if her life depended on choosing the right bun or pastry.

'Two cinnamon rolls,' she said at last, raising her eyes.

'Cinnamon rolls it is,' Marianne jovially replied as she placed two big buns sprinkled with sugar on two separate plates.

'My husband would prefer the kind without the powdered sugar,' said Eva Wärn, casting a hasty look over her shoulder at the man sitting near the window.

Marianne didn't say a word, merely raised an

eyebrow as tiny scraps of information began whirling through her head. After exchanging the buns for ones with sliced almonds on top, she studied the woman more closely than she had before. That tired, worn-out look that she'd noticed the first time they met was still there. Along with something else. And now she couldn't understand how she'd missed it before. What she saw in Eva Wärn's face was . . . herself.

Marianne placed her hand on the inspector's and said in a gentle voice, 'And what would you like to drink?'

For a moment Eva Wärn didn't speak as she stared at the hand resting on top of her own. Then she raised her eyes and said in a firm voice:

'A caffe latte for me. And a Widow's Special for my husband.'

Marianne looked her in the eye for a long moment. Then she turned and began preparing the order.